Pablo's Ghost

Strike Force X: Book One

MICHAEL NEWTON

WOLFPACK
PUBLISHING
— EST 2013 —

WOLFPACK
PUBLISHING
— EST 2013 —

Paperback Edition
Copyright © 2020 Michael Newton

Published in the United States by Wolfpack Publishing, Las Vegas

Wolfpack Publishing
6032 Wheat Penny Avenue
Las Vegas, NV 89122

wolfpackpublishing.com

Paperback ISBN 978-1-64734-895-3
Kindle ISBN 978-1-64734-894-6

Library of Congress Number: 2020940906

Pablo's Ghost

For E.T. and Mackenzie

"I have always considered myself a happy man. I've always been happy, I've always been optimistic, I've always had faith in life because I think the most difficult times always bring something. It brings experience, and it's the greatest thing to have in life."

Pablo Escobar

"All empires are created of blood and fire."

Pablo Escobar

1

Antioquia Department, Colombia

An unseen hand ripped the black linen hood from off Rogelio Vélez's bruised and bloodied head, causing his rodentlike eyes to squint against the sudden glare of ceiling-mounted floodlights. Pain, a constant since the moment he had been abducted, flared to agony inside his skull.

Vélez tried to survey his prison, which by all apparent indicators—smell, sound, sight as he regained it—seemed to be an old, disused warehouse abandoned to the pigeons, rats and spiders that lay claim to such former abodes of men. A forklift layered with years of dust sat at the far end of the massive chamber. Small things scratched and scuttled in its dark corners.

Beside Vélez, immediately to his left, was Andrés Araújo, blinking as if to mimic his employer, drying blood caked on lips and chin as if it were a rusty-colored Van Dyke beard. Both men were handcuffed, wrists secured behind their backs. Beyond that, both were bound with thin, tough nylon ropes to painfully uncomfortable metal folding chairs.

It was outrageous for such men of prominence to be abused this way. If Vélez was not living it, he might have called the travesty unthinkable.

He and Araújo had been leaving the Agujero de la Gloria nightclub in Parque Lleras, Medellín's center of action between dusk and dawn, accompanied by young cabaret dancers, when a black van screeched to a halt beside Vélez's silver limousine, disgorging six armed men dressed all in black from balaclavas down to combat boots, shouting commands for everyone to raise their hands.

Vélez's driver earned his pay by reaching for the pistol in his shoulder holster. One of the attackers dropped him with a three-round burst of submachine-gun fire. Another set the women running for their lives—an awkward flight in tall stiletto heels—while the remaining four frisked Vélez and Araújo, handcuffed them, and dragged them both inside the van, where hoods were snugged over their heads. When each in turn asked what was happening, who the abductors thought they were, they had been gun-whipped into silence.

Now here they were, wherever *here* might be, trussed up and staring at a forklift, half a dozen wooden pallets, and a rat creeping along the nearest wall.

But they were not alone.

Although the watchers made no sound, Vélez trusted his finely-honed survival sense to tell him that much.

What a pity that it was unlikely to preserve his life much longer. There could be no coming back from this sort of intrusion, such a mortal insult. Logic and experience told him he could only end up with a shallow grave—or worse.

Behind him, a man's voice said, "So, we meet again, Rogelio."

Footsteps on cracked concrete approached him from behind, then moved around Araújo's chair. The speaker stood before them, smiling almost wistfully. His face was instantly familiar, although changed somewhat by time and circumstance, but recognizable. Stunning.

"You're dead," Vélez half-whispered. "Dead for what? How many years?"

"Approaching twenty-eight," the man behind their kidnapping replied. "But who's counting?"

"This is impossible," Vélez declared, trying for greater strength and emphasis.

"And yet…"

The dead man spread his hands, stepped closer, bending from the waist to let Vélez survey his face up close and personal. Same wavy hair, still black on top but with more gray around the temples. Same thick eyebrows. Same bushy mustache as in the early mugshots, later in the media. The smile beneath that mugshot still projected mockery.

"Rogelio, do you not trust your own two eyes?"

"I saw your body," said Vélez. "I was among the mourners at your funeral…"

"You dare not speak my name?" the dead man challenged him.

"It *can't* be you."

"Perhaps this will convince you, then."

The man who couldn't be stepped closer, bending from the waist, and raised a hand to brush the graying hair back from his right temple. Vélez beheld the dimpled scar there, felt the warehouse and his whole world tilting.

"Pablo Emilio?"

Having presented his stigmata for inspection, their kidnapper straightened and stepped back a pace. His smile beneath the famous mustache morphed into a frown.

"At last," he said. "It grieves me to inform you of my disappointment."

"What? I don't—"

"*La Oficina de Envigado*, Rogelio."

"Yes? And?"

Before the Medellín Cartel's collapse in 1993, Vélez

had organized the so-called "Office of Envigado"—a town located seven miles southwest of Antioquia Department's capital in the Aburrá Valley. Formed as a defense against the cartel's enemies in Cali and the wild men of Los Pepes— short for "*per*secuted by *P*ablo *Es*cobar"—it had fought on to the bitter end, then managed to survives as a successor syndicate of sorts, maintaining ties to both the government in Bogotá and to guerillas lurking in the hinterlands.

"You organized us, Pablo," said Vélez, still nearly choking on the name. "We followed your instructions to the letter, did whatever you commanded."

"Until you believed that I was gone," their host responded in a scolding tone. "Since then you've made yourself a multi-millionaire and man of influence. Is that not so, Rogelio?"

"I carried on," Vélez protested, "and survived. I never slighted you—your memory—by any word or deed."

"Unless we count attempting to control my former territory, eh?" The not-so-dead man shrugged and spread his hands. "But what of that? Time passes. Life moves on."

For some, Vélez thought, but he kept it to himself.

"The good news, now, is that I'm back!" his captor said, smiling again. "I am reclaiming all that's mine and all that would have been, if traitors had not stabbed me in the back."

"You can't mean—"

"What else *could* I mean?" the image of a man long dead replied. "Do you expect me to believe the Search Bloc and Los Pepes actually traced my phone to Los Olivos and surprised me there, among my own people who loved me, owed me everything they had, from homes and hospital to schools and churches, plus their daily bread? Do you accept the lie that I grew frightened near the end and shot myself to keep from going back to prison? Eh?"

"But—"

"No!" The voice rose to a shout. "We both know who bears the responsibility. Is that now true, Rogelio?"

"You think that *I* betrayed you?" Vélez could no longer feign a pose of disbelief. His mind could not conceive how such a thing was possible, and yet...

"I think nothing," the man who had returned to life answered. "I know it for a fact. A certainty."

"You are mistaken, *jefe*."

"Don't debase yourself with any further lies. You have been tried, convicted, and your sentence passed. You know what must be done to halt contagion's spread."

Vélez could think of no response, sat blinking at his former lord and master, now become his mortal enemy.

The ghost made flesh pressed on. "It must be purged by fire."

Rogelio Vélez stared blankly at the man standing before him. He could feel Andrés Araújo staring at him, but kept his eyes fixed directly on the man in charge.

"What does that mean, Pablo?"

Forcing the name between his bloodied lips left Vélez with a foul taste in his mouth.

Instead of answering, his captor looked beyond his prisoners and raised his right hand, snapped his fingers some other watchers who had been observing the proceedings from behind Vélez and his lieutenant, staying silent, out of sight.

On cue, two men Vélez had never seen before stepped into sight, one to his right, the other passing by Araújo on the left. Although the men were strangers, Vélez recognized the type. They were *sicarios*—hired killers—both in their mid-twenties, dressed in track suits and expensive running shoes. Each carried a red plastic gasoline container in one hand, the usual five-gallon size.

"Treason shall be expunged," their leader said. "Eradicated. Only ashes of betrayal will remain."

He nodded, and the silent hitmen both removed the twist caps from their fuel containers, tossing them aside. As one, they stepped forward, raising the plastic jerrycans, prepared to dump their contents on the seated prisoners.

"Wait!" Vélez cried, hating the tremor in his voice. "Don't do this, Pablo!"

"You pretend I have a choice, Rogelio," his judge and would-be executioner replied. "How often have you done this very thing, or worse, while you pretended to safeguard my interests?"

"I swear to Jesus Christ above that I have not betrayed you, *jefe*!"

"Save your breath for Him," the man in charge replied. "Assuming He will deign to speak with you." Then, speaking to his men, "Proceed!"

Vélez was gagging on the fumes of high-test gasoline before the man assigned to him began pouring the fuel over his head. Eyes shut against the reeking deluge, Vélez gasped as it awakened fresh pain from his facial gashes— nothing, he knew all too well, compared with what would follow soon.

Beside him, Vélez heard Araújo vomiting, spewing some of the alcohol he had consumed within the hour, give or take, at the Agujero de la Gloria, when he believed this night would end with sweaty sex on satin sheets. Fighting an urge to follow suit, Vélez cried out instead.

"Please reconsider, Pablo! It is not too late!"

"For you, it is. The choice was yours." Then, to his men, "*¡Encederlos!*"

Vélez could only close his eyes and lips against the coming holocaust. He heard cheap lighters thumbed to life before one clattered at his feet, the other near Araújo's. Still, there was no blocking out the flames, their searing heat, as flames erupted from his hair, his flesh and clothing.

For a split-second, Vélez recalled advice he had received from some old cartel warrior years before. "If you are ever trapped by fire and can't escape," his mentor in those by-gone days cautioned, "face toward the flames and breathe as deeply as you can, to sear your lungs and hasten death."

But now, blazing from scalp down to his seven hundred-dollar handmade shoes, all that Rogelio Velez could do was scream.

2

Dzanga-Sangha Special Reserve, Central African Republic

Reg Hardy scanned the tree line thought his Steyer AUG's Swarovski 1.5× telescopic sight, watching for movement in the shadows there.

The Austrian assault rifle ranked high on Hardy's list of favorites. A bullpup design with its magazine slotted behind the pistol grip and trigger, it chambered 5.56×45mm NATO rounds and fed them with selective-fire capability ranging from single shots to three-round bursts or fully automatic fire. Translucent magazines allowed a shooter to determine his remaining ammo with a glance. The weapon weighed a trifle under eight pounds, measured 31.1 inches from its muzzles flash suppressor to the butt plate of its shoulder stock, and qualified for service with thirty-five armies and seventeen major law enforcement agencies worldwide.

Today, accompanied by four veterans of FACA—the Central African Armed Forces—Hardy was prepared to intercept a group of poachers who had plagued the government and its endangered wildlife far too long.

The unit did not plan on taking any prisoners. The Dzanga-Sangha Reserve, established in 1990, sprawls over 1,544 square miles of rainforest in the southwestern

CAR. Ecologically rich, it harbors more than fifty species of mammals, many under threat of imminent extinction, plus an estimated 2,500 Baka natives dwelling as their forebears had during the Stone Age. Wildlife tourism at the reserve boosts the CAR's weak economy, but it still ranks among the world's poorest nations, where employed citizens earn an average $400 per year.

The reserve also supports a thriving black market for poachers, particularly stalking western lowland gorillas, shot and dismembered for ghoulish "souvenirs," and forest elephants slaughtered for ivory.

Today, Reg Hardy had the pachyderms in mind.

Forest elephants are the smallest of Earth's three surviving species, noted for oval-shaped ears and straighter, downward-pointing tusks than those of their larger relatives in Africa and Asia. Living in family groups of twenty-odd individuals, they contribute greatly to the Dark Continent's rain forests, foraging on leaves, fruit, and tree bark, nicknamed "mega-gardeners of the forest," replenishing natural flora with seeds and pits passed through the elephants' digestive tracts.

That is, if they survived.

Poachers cared about nothing but money. International bans on ivory sales had the same effect as Prohibition had on alcohol, or global drug laws on trafficking in controlled chemicals. On one recent occasion, poachers had massacred an entire herd of twenty-six forest elephants, carting off the tusks, leaving their carcasses to rot.

Reg Hardy's hand-picked team sought to accord those butchers the precise respect which they accorded to their prey.

Forget about negotiation and "tough love." Across the so-called "Third World" justice was a stone-cold bitch.

Hardy focused and froze. Softly advised his men, "Movement at ten o'clock."

Emerging from the shadows, half a dozen men in camouflaged fatigues, all armed with rifles, edged into the open. Ranged around Hardy, his men sighted along the barrels of their Russian AKM assault weapons.

"Ready," he said, then squeezed the Steyr's trigger, reaching out across one hundred yards to drop the central figure in the poachers' skirmish line.

Short bursts of auto fire from his companions did the rest. Surprised, a couple of the poachers got off random shots but did no damage to the ambush team. Within a span of ninety seconds all of them were down and out for good. Hardy felt nothing in the aftermath of sudden mayhem other than the satisfaction of a job well done.

No questions would be asked in Bangui, the CAR's capital city. No one among the thirty-one appointees to the CAR's Council of Ministers cared what went on in the hinterlands, as long as they could plausibly preserve deniability. Hardy's contract was strictly off the books, permitting any ministers who'd taken payoffs from a poaching network or illicit buyers to retain the cash with no fear of demands for a refund. This time next week, they'd likely have another source of bribes lined up and Hardy adjust his sights for those offenders.

Hardy led his companions over open ground to form a ring around their fallen enemies. One of the poachers was still moaning, moving fitfully. An AKM round ended that.

"So, shall we bury them?" one of his young companions asked.

"Negative," Hardy said. "We'll take their weapons with us. Otherwise, leopards and vultures need to eat, the same as worms."

The roam phone in his pocket shivered silently. Hardy removed it, saw the number on its LED screen, keyed "ACCEPT" to take the call. Said, "What?"

"We have a job, if you're available," the caller answered back.

"Same place?"

"The usual."

"I should be there sometime tomorrow."

"See you then."

Bucharest, Romania

The Paradise Hotel had never lived up to its name.

For starters, it was situated in the Ferentari district, ranked on most lists as the capital's worst neighborhood for crime and drugs, though it was located a mere three miles southwest of bustling, thriving downtown Bucharest. In Ferentari, alleyways and vacant lots were heaped with garbage that no city agency bothered to haul away. Armed gangs patrolled the narrow, littered streets, fighting sporadically for turf, most selling cocaine, heroin, or any other outlawed drug they did not privately consume.

None of that concerned Natalie Karpin as she stood on Strada Anghel Dogaru, directly opposite the misnamed Paradise Hotel. She had no interest in drugs or gangs today, much less in sanitation.

She was looking for a tourist—an American, from New York City—who had traveled some five thousand miles at great expense to wallow in debauchery.

No prude herself, Karpin had certain lines she would not cross, nor tolerate the felonies of others when she had an opportunity to cut them short.

One such offender was Stuart Delaney, a successful Wall Street lawyer living on his own in the Dakota Apartments on Central Park West, in Manhattan's Upper West Side. He was unmarried, seldom entertained at home, and kept his nose clean on the public record—no small feat, considering that he was what psychiatrists would call a pedophile.

Natalie Karpin had no patience with the jargon tossed around by shrinks and lawyers representing clients who found it impossible to stop molesting, raping, sometimes even killing children in pursuit of psychopathic sexual release. She knew the textbook definition of pedophilia called it "a psychiatric disorder in which an adult or adolescent experiences a primary sexual attraction to prepubescent children," but she was not concerned with anyone's attraction to another person, animal or some inanimate object.

When they crossed the line from lusting into predatory action there could be no turning back.

Police did what they could to keep that plague in check, but some transgressors were simply beyond their league. Stuart Delaney earned an average four million dollars yearly from his legal practice, without adding in the laundered dividends received from offshore banks. He took six weeks' vacation during most years, traveling the world to visit nations where sex with children had been banned by law but government corruption meant such crimes were tolerated with a wink and nod if tourists and rich locals amply greased local authorities.

Delaney alternated jet-set traveling between Cuzco in Peru, Bangkok, Thailand and Bucharest, depending on the season and prevailing weather. This time he was in Romania and booked into the Paradise, a long way down the social scale from Manhattan co-op overlooking Central Park.

If Karpin had her way, this would be the attorney's final trip abroad and his next transatlantic flight would find him in a Boeing 747's cargo hold, securely bolted in a casket.

She knew Delaney was inside the Paradise, a spartan room on the third floor, waiting for Iosif Brâncuşi, a scumbag pimp, to make delivery of one boy in the range of six to eight years old. For two hours alone with his intended victim, the attorney would be shelling out 62,000 Romanian leu, equivalent to $15,000 U.S.

That was no small fortune in a country where the average worker with a college degree earned just over $500 per year before taxes.

But today, with any luck, Delaney and Brâncuşi would be going out of business. Back in Gotham, IRS agents would pick over Delaney's leavings, while in Bucharest, surviving bottom-feeders would carve up Brâncuşi's trade and any cash he hadn't spent feeding his methamphetamine habit.

Again, Natalie Karpin didn't give a damn.

She crossed the street, waded through garbage in an alley on the north side of the Paradise, and entered through the hotel's backdoor once she lockpicked its cheap deadbolt. Inside, she put the pick away and drew a Glock 17M pistol, the same model issued to FBI agents stateside, chambered in 9×19mm Parabellum, with seventeen rounds in the mag and one in the chamber. Unlike the Bureau's guns, this one had an extended muzzle, threaded to accommodate a sound suppressor that added one-third to the gun's loaded weight of two pounds.

Natalie climbed the service stairs and found room 313 halfway along a dingy corridor with half the ceiling lights burned out. That seemed to fit, given the kind of business normally conducted at the Paradise. There was no peephole in the door that would permit its tenant to observe her in the hall.

Natalie knocked and waited. The door opened to reveal Stuart Delaney, forty-four years old and looking every second of it, blinking at her in surprise. "Wrong room," he said, mangling the tourist guidebook phrase, and was about to shut the door when Karpin raised her Glock and shot him in the face.

No fuss and very little muss.

She dragged him toward the middle of a living room whose central feature was a double bed. The other furniture consisted of a small, chipped dresser and a single straight-backed wooden chair. She closed and latched the door, ignored

Delaney's leaking corpse, and sat down in the chair to wait.

The best part of an hour passed before another visitor knocked on the door to 313 It had to be Iosif Brâncuşi, since the Paradise had no room service and a maid would not appear until the tenant had checked out, no matter how long he or she remained. The no-frills dump provided handy crime scenes, charging by the hour what a reputable place downtown might charge per night, and few of those who used its services were overly concerned with hygiene.

Rising, Karpin stepped around Delaney's body to the door, released its deadbolt, opened it and edged back to remain concealed from the latest arrivals.

Brâncuşi entered first, leading a small boy by the hand. The pimp saw Natalie, blanched at the pistol in her hand, his client on the floor, then died with an amazed expression on his sallow face, blood pumping from a vent above his left eyebrow. The child fled and she made no effort to restrain him, heard him pounding down the stairs as she wiped down the inner doorknob to remove her fingerprints.

Romanian police weren't much on scientific crime-fighting, but even they knew basic methods and attempted the solution of a felony from time to time, if that seemed feasible.

As for the boy, Natalie reckoned she'd done all that she could do under the circumstances. Each year, some 1.2 million children were trafficked worldwide. Nearly one-fifth of those were smuggled out of Eastern Europe, a "significant proportion" from Romania, according to United Nations documents. Her work today would not have solved that problem, obviously, but it was a baby-step. Investigation of Brâncuşi's murder, if police applied themselves at all, might turn over some larger stones and bare the maggots wriggling underneath.

Karpin had nearly reached her rental car when her roam phone buzzed on her hip. She recognized the caller's number, answered on the second ring. "What's up?"

"Are you available?"

"I can be. Where and when?"

"Same place. Tomorrow suit you?"

"On my way," she said, and cut the link.

Houston, Texas

The sports arena was not average, nothing on par with the Sam Houston Coliseum, the Toyota Center or the Alexander Durley Sports Complex. It was, in fact, a renovated warehouse in Galena Park, a couple blocks from Buffalo Bayou.

The kind of place you might expect to watch an MMA cage match with no holds barred.

Blake Mahoney wasn't rated as a headliner. In fact, he wasn't on the card at all, per se. When he pursued mixed martial arts for profit or simply for the excitement of it, he appeared as "Michael Blake," no fixed address that any of the bettors and spectators knew or cared about. He'd been approached on one occasion by a bookie, offering a grand if he would throw a fight where he was favored as the winner, but he'd punched the asshole into traction and advised him to report it as a traffic hit-and-run.

If anyone had ever tried to follow up on that, no word of it had reached Mahoney at his home in San Diego. Woe betide whoever tried to track him down for that, or any indiscretion from his past, unconscious of the Hell they would bring down upon themselves.

His opposition on the undercard tonight was Clemente Arredando out of Dallas, shorter than Mahoney at five foot eleven but nearly equal in weight at one-ninety. His body was a canvas of tattoos, something like *The Illustrated Man* by Ray Bradbury or demigod Maui in that Walt Disney animated film where Dwayne Johnson proved that he could sing. Each time he flexed, it seemed as if a painter's sketch-book came alive, and that could be distracting in the cage.

If his opponent paid attention, anyway.

Mahoney ducked distractions, concentrating on the other grappler's eyes, his hands and feet. Most fighters telegraphed their moves somehow, whether intending to or not, and if you trained yourself to spot those tells, it went a long way toward a knockout.

Arredando held black belts in Shotokan karate, Tae-kwando and Aikido, but none of that made him invincible. He bled and suffered pain like anybody else. The trick was to deliver more than he could handle in as short a time as possible and get the whole thing over with.

They shook hands, Arredondo tossing in a sneer he meant to be intimidating, then backed off from one an-other, waiting for the first round's bell to sound. It rang, and Blake Mahoney flew toward Arredondo with a storm of kicks and punches that were swift enough to drive his enemy backward, on the defensive, landing blows on either of Mahoney's shoulders that would bruise but cause no lasting damage. When he put his weight behind the final one-two punch that blacked out Arredondo's lights, a hush fell on the audience, then broke into a wave of cheers from those who'd put their money on the white guy.

From the others, not so much.

Mahoney's phone was buzzing when he got back to his locker. Opening the padlock, he reached in and fished it out. "Good timing, Bro," he said.

"You want in on a job?" the caller asked.

"Will there be traveling?"

"Oh, yeah."

"Not nowhere cold?"

"Not this time."

"When?"

"Tomorrow at the usual?"

"Okay. I'm in."

Las Vegas, Nevada

"Las Vegas" is a Spanish phrase that translated into English as "the meadows, as its state—Nevada—means "snow-clad." Both were derived from first impressions of late 18th-century explorers from New Spain, later rechristened Mexico. Prospectors came along in time, sank shafts, and dubbed the territory that they called their own the "Silver State."

Successive waves of interlopers had been looting the Nevada desert ever since.

Las Vegas was a tawdry wide spot in the road until the end of World War II, when mobsters from the New York and elsewhere realized that back in 1931, state legislators tried to save their state from the Depression by legalizing gambling and granting quickie divorces. Drug money poured in, building lavish "carpet joints" to squeeze out mom-and-pop casinos catering to cowboys who spent more time playing cards or shooting craps than showering or polishing their boots. The first pirates to land were mostly Jewish or Italian—men like Bugsy Siegel, Meyer Lansky, Frank Costello and Sam Giancana.

Nowadays, they might be anyone from anywhere on Earth.

Money still talked in Vegas, and most inhabitants were good at listening. Most also had their hands out, one way or another, for whatever scraps the "whales" might leave behind.

It was a whole new Mob these days—or *mobs,* more properly—from Russia, Eastern Europe, Southeast Asia, all over the globe, in fact. Tonight there was a merger in the making, fat cats gathered in the penthouse of the King's Ransom resort downtown, on Glitter Gulch, an alias for Fremont Street.

The rivalry amounting to a blood feud had persisted between China and Japan over two millennia and change, as far back as reliable recorded history. That's gotten worse since World War II, with China going Red while Washington remade Japan in its own capitalist image. That discord had also been reflected in their separate crime syndicates. The Yakuza, with four dominant families, was subdivided into some 300 smaller clans with forty thousand members estimated globally. The Chinese Triads, ruled by seven families, also claimed roughly forty thousand oath-bound members, working in conjunction with at least nineteen affiliated gangs worldwide.

Both had their outposts in Las Vegas, had been present in "Sin City" since the 1980s if not earlier, but from reports Dartnell had recently obtained, tonight would be their first attempt to merge—unless, somehow, it all went suddenly, disastrously wrong.

He meant to see it do exactly that.

Security was tight at the King's Ransom, as at all legal casinos in Nevada. Guards in uniform were supplemented by an equal number in plainclothes, all armed, while video surveillance teams—the gaming industry's famous "eyes in the sky" peered down from mirrored ceilings, equally alert for cheaters, random thieves, minors intruding on the glitzy world with fake I.D.s, and armed invaders from outside who might try anything from holdups to a targeted assassination.

Nothing had been left to chance, but those in charge had failed to take account of Stan Dartnell.

He knew when and where the meeting would be held, at 8:00 p.m. in the hotel's executive conference room, one floor below the presidential suite that hadn't seen a chief executive check in so far. Security would be divided up between the Yakuza and Triad factions, but Dartnell had no concerns about making his way inside.

Whether he left the room alive, however, was another question altogether.

He was well armed for the sortie, starting with a Mini-Uzi submachine gun and a dozen magazines loaded with forty rounds of 9×19mm Parabellum ammunition each. The sleek Beretta M9 semiautomatic pistol in his horizontal Jackass shoulder holster fed the same ammo from magazines containing fifteen rounds apiece. Clipped to his belt beneath his jacket, just in case it all went south, Dartnell had four M67 fragmentation hand grenades, each with a lethal radius of sixteen feet and wounding range three times that distance.

He was good to go.

Stan rode the elevator up to level nine and left it there, using the fire stairs to complete his journey without tipping off the guards too soon. Once they accosted him, the shit would then become extremely real and there would be no turning back. He'd either pull it off and slip away, or else he'd leave the King's Ransom zipped up inside a rubber body bag.

He'd been unable to devise a third alternative.

On level ten, he cracked the metal fire door, peeked into the corridor, and found four guards on duty there, two Japanese, the other pair Chinese. Not being one of those benighted souls who claimed all Asians "look alike," he had no trouble differentiating them.

He double-checked the Uzi without needing to and was about to show himself when buzzing in his jacket's right-hand pocket made him hesitate. He checked the roam phone, mouthed a silent curse, and answered, "What?"

"I catch you at a bad time?"

"Just a little busy," he replied.

"I've got a job lined up, you want to come on board?"

"When would it start?"

"Meeting tomorrow with the team, same place as usual."

"I'll be there if I can," Dartnell agreed. "But if I miss it, go ahead without me."

"Right. Okay. We'll hope to see you there."

Dartnell switched off the phone without goodbyes, replaced it in his pocket, and stepped out into the hotel corridor. Four pairs of eyes immediately locked upon him and the automatic weapon in his hands.

"Yo, boys!" he called out cheerily. "Am I too late for appetizers?"

All four went for hidden pistols and he held the Uzi's trigger down.

3

The headquarters of SFX Corporation stands on the east side of Fifth Avenue between Broadway and E Street, two and one-half miles southwest of San Diego's famous zoo in Balboa Park. On quiet nights, if one of those should roll around, locals claim they can hear the big cats roaring in their various enclosures.

Or perhaps that's only wishful thinking.

SFX is something of a mystery to other business owners on the block. Most casually know or recognize on sight its CEO, one Grant Mahoney, and they've seen his younger brother come and go from time to time, but none could tell you what the corporation does to stay in business and support its pricey digs.

Some speculate that SFX is in the movie business, possibly computer-generated imagery, since "SFX" is Hollywood-speak for special effects, but none can say they've ever seen a film or TV star hanging around the premises. The firm solicits no inquiries from potential customers, and no one can recall it ever advertising for employee applications. People come and go, of course, but they are generally nondescript and readily forgettable.

The Gaslamp Quarter—or the Gaslamp District, as

locals insist, defying public presentation on its entry arch and all official city signage—covers sixteen and one-half blocks downtown, boasting several entertainment and nightlife venues, plus various seasonal festivals. Petco Park, home of the San Diego Padres, stands one block outside the district in San Diego's East Village. Developed from 1867 onward, the Quarter includes ninety-four buildings erected during the Victorian Era, earning the neighborhood's listing in the National Register of Historic Places. Tourists flock there, and to San Diego generally, but you'll find no visitors in gaudy clothes or school bus tours stopping off at SFX.

Sitting behind his desk, inside the headquarters, CEO and cofounder Grant Mahoney frowned over his copy of the *San Diego Tribune*, finishing an article whose headline read "Asian Gang Shootout in Las Vegas." The details were sparse, aside from a report of seven dead and four in custody, detained as material witnesses to multiple murders. None were named, but the *Tribune*'s anonymous reporter wrote that all involved were either Japanese or Chinese, theoretically connected to the Yakuza or Triads operating out of Hong Kong.

This appeared to be one time when what happened in Vegas wasn't staying there.

"Something catch your attention?" asked his visitor.

"Nothing to do with me," Mahoney answered, keeping to himself the thought that followed: *But it may be tied to somebody I know.*

Someone who ought to be arriving soon.

Mahoney had selected San Diego as the home for SFX in part because the city's climate ranked as second-best in the United States according to the Weather Channel and among America's top ten from *Farmer's Almanac*. Its temperature rarely dipped below 50° Fahrenheit in January or exceeded 78° in mid-August. Granted, there were times when thick "marine air" clouds besieged the coast, imposing "May gray/June gloom" interludes, but nothing that unduly troubled zoo inhabitants or tourists.

Yet another selling point was San Diego County's role as economic centerpiece of Southern California, with proximity to the Mexican border as heart of the San Diego-Tijuana metropolitan area. To that milieu of tourism and international trade, add the University of California, San Diego, with its affiliated UCSD Medical Center, making the area a center of biotechnology research. In 2014 *Forbes* magazine ranked San Diego as America's best place to launch a small business or startup company.

Finally, a major portion of the region's thriving economy hinged upon military and defense-related activities, linchpins of SFX's *raison d'être*. The U.S. Navy operated Naval Base San Diego, homeport to the Pacific Fleet; Assault Craft Unit One; the Naval Surface Warfare Center; and the Navy Sealift Command Center, among others. Camp Pendleton is the Marine Corps' largest West Coast base of operations, backed up by Marine Corps Air Base Miramar and Naval Amphibious Base Coronado. The Air Force and Coast Guard, likewise, are well represented. The U.S. Army, on the light side in "Dago," still maintained a large Healthcare Recruiting Center, while a field office of the Defense Contract Audit Agency ostensibly kept close watch on the watchmen. Other agencies assigned to safeguard the nation include the Drug Enforcement Administration, the FBI, Homeland Security, the Border Patrol and other long arms of law enforcement, state, county and local.

Mahoney's visitor glanced at his watch and frowned. The timepiece looked like a black-dial Rolex Submariner, retailing around eleven grand, but it would have to be a knockoff—that is, if his guest was operating on the up-and-up, without padding his salary from some illicit source. Grant slotted that away, deciding it might rate further investigation if their project went ahead.

"Where are these guys that I'm supposed to meet?" his first-time visitor inquired, just as a faint chime from the outer hallway heralded an elevator car's arrival.

"That should be one of them now," Mahoney said. "But brace yourself. They're not all guys."

"You don't mean…"

"Wait and see," Mahoney said. "If you don't like the team, that door you came in through can take you right back out again."

In fact, the first team member through the door at SFX wasn't a "guy" by any stretch of the imagination. Grant Mahoney raised a hand to her, said, "Hey, Nat," while she took a moment to size up the stranger.

"Who's this?" Natalie Karpin inquired.

"I'll introduce him soon as everybody's here."

Not giving any names away, she said, "The rest of them are all downstairs."

Over the next five minutes, give or take, the SFX team's final trio entered. All of them were guys indeed, the last one taking time to lock the office door's interior deadbolt while he was studying the stranger in their midst.

The next to enter after Natalie, Grant's younger brother Blake, was cofounder of SFX and partner in the firm, though he left most of the daily operations to his sibling. They'd been friendly rivals for the most part, all their lives, competing with each other from to selection of the military branches they had served with—Delta Force for Grant, Blake with the Navy SEALS—but when their parents died together in an Arizona car crash, both sons, on deployment at the time, rushed home to meet at graveside, they'd agreed in principle that it was time to work together for a change. Settling the details and retiring from the military had required some time and unfamiliar compromise, but they were at the helm of SFX today.

Reginald Hardy was a Brit and veteran of Her Majesty's Special Air Service, known for its classified engagements on a par with Delta and the SEALs. He was the team's "old man" at forty, born on April first, and liked to say that his arrival was an April Fool's Day joke that Fate had played on his unwitting parents. They had wanted him to be a doctor or attorney, but he'd never made it into college, much less grad school. Six feet tall and stocky, with green eyes and prematurely graying hair, he'd been a crack commando with the SAS and designated marksman—what civilians and reporters liked to call a sniper. A native English speaker, he was also fluent in German, Cantonese, Mandarin and Swahili.

Stanley Dartnell hailed from Down Under, second oldest of the SFX team, six foot two and some fifteen pounds lighter than Hardy's two hundred. He kept his head shaved but sometimes donned a wig if the job didn't fit skinhead chic. Before he joined the SFX team, Stan had risen to captain's rank with the Australia Defense Force's Special Operations Command, equivalent to the other elite fighting units his colleagues had served. Aside from English with an Aussie accent, he spoke Korean, Malay, Tagalog and French.

Last but certainly not least by any means, Nat Karpin, twenty-nine years old, was an Israeli-born sabra who'd performed her national service and then some with Sayeret Matkal, which translated from Hebrew to English as the Special Reconnaissance Force of her homeland's General Staff. Fluent in five languages, she was expert with small arms and explosives, and a stone-cold master of krav maga "dirty" fighting who could probably match Blake Mahoney blow for blow if they'd been thrown together in a cage.

When all of them were seated around SFX's conference table, Grant Mahoney introduced the stranger they'd been eyeballing with frank suspicion. "People, this is Preston Chandler from the DEA," he told them.

"Just say now," jibed brother Blake, grinning.

"If only that would get it done," Chandler replied. "Unfortunately, in the real world—"

"Tell us all about it, mate," Dartnell chimed in.

"Let's hear him out," their CEO suggested. "You might find it…interesting."

"Go ahead, then," Blake spoke for the rest.

Preston continued, speaking through a frown. "I take it that you've heard of Pablo Escobar," he said.

"Old guy who used to run the Medellín Cartel," said Natalie.

"Old *dead* guy," Blake Mahoney added. "What's it been, like thirty years?"

"Almost," said Preston. "That's assuming that he *is* dead."

Hardy barked a laugh at that. "Are you taking the piss, old son? Some of us were around to see him killed on CNN."

"And yet," Preston replied, "today we're getting word that he may be alive and well, up to his same old tricks and trying for a comeback."

"If that were true," Nat challenged him, "he'd be an old man now."

"Born in December 1949," said Preston. "Coming up on his seventy-second birthday."

"If we just ignore that pesky point-blank head shot," Dartnell said.

"Ignoring that for now," the DEA man answered back. "The thing is, he'd been seen by folks who knew him well. They claim he's back, and not decrepit like you'd think. Younger, some of them say, around the age he would have been when he supposedly went down at Los Olivos."

"Someone's feeding you a line, mate," Dartnell said.

Preston was nodding. "That's what I thought, too. It's what headquarters thought the first couple of times the rumors surfaced. Then it started getting real."

"How real?" Blake asked.

"Somebody's picking off his former enemies—the ones who weren't in prison or the grave before this started," Preston said. "More recently, they've started taking out some characters who used to be his friends."

"Such as?" Hardy inquired.

"The latest, just last week, were the head operators of *La Oficina de Envigado*, if you know what that is."

"We're familiar with it," Grant assured him.

"Okay. Somebody snatched its leader and his top lieutenant as they left a club in Medellín. A phone call sent the National Police out to a warehouse in Manrique—that's a Medellín suburb—where they were found handcuffed to chairs and burned alive."

"Remind me to feel sorry for them later," Blake suggested.

Preston ignored that. Told them, "What the DEA is asking, what we need, is for some private contractors to check it out, report back on whatever's happening before it blows up in our faces any worse."

"And you don't trust the law down there," Natalie said, not asking it.

"Who would?" Preston replied. "We're on thin ice with Bogotá as usual." He turned to Grant, asking, "So, are you in or out?"

"We need to talk about it privately," Mahoney said.

After another quick look at his maybe-Rolex, Preston said, "I need an answer by tonight."

"You'll have it," Grant said, "one way or another."

"No later than midnight, or we'll have to call somebody else."

"No problem. Now, if you'll excuse us…"

"He doesn't like us," Natalie observed, when they were rid of Preston.

Grant told them all the obvious. "Nobody with a badge likes private military contractors. They need us, though, when they get through pretending they can do it all themselves and stay within the law."

"Forget the fuzzy feelings," brother Blake put in. "He's DEA. I wouldn't trust him if his tongue came notarized."

"It's what we do, though," Grant replied. "That is, if we agree to take it on."

"It sounds like shite to me," Hardy opined. "Some kind of old wives' tale or urban legend, take your pick."

"Don't know old wives," said Natalie. "And some legends are based on fact."

Blake snorted. "So, the King of Cocaine is a zombie now? It's crap, like Reg said. Has to be."

"That's not the question," Grant reminded them. "The DEA's just asking us to find out and report back."

"From Colombia," Dartnell reminded him. "The goddamn place has been a war zone since the last World War."

"And we've been there before," Grant said. "We made it back in one piece, right?"

"Why push our luck chasing a fairy tale?" his brother asked.

"You haven't asked about the money yet," Grant answered back.

"Okay. Enlighten us," his brother said.

"Two million, plus expenses. After putting half back into SFX, that leaves—"

"Two hundred grand apiece," Blake finished for him.

"Right. On top of which, Preston is offering local support."

"His own men on the ground?" Natalie asked. "Can't say I like the sound of that."

"He didn't, either," Grant advised. "They have a local man in Medellín helping them out. I've got his name and contact info if we take the job."

"Colombian," Blake groused. "That makes me trust him even less."

"We'd have to vet him, obviously," Grant replied. "However many hoops he has to jump through, Preston is amenable."

"I'd bet somebody said the same to Kiki Camarena," Blake responded.

Enrique "Kiki" Camarena was a DEA agent in Mexico who'd been kidnapped and tortured to death by members of the Guadalajara Cartel, launching a blood feud that destroyed that syndicate four years later, leaving the rival Gulf Cartel to pick up the remnants and inaugurate Mexico's ongoing drug war, costing some 150,000 lives on both sides at the last estimate, with no end in sight.

"Easy to die down there," Natalie told the room.

"Easy to die on any job we take," Grant countered. "If we get down there and don't think we can handle it, we'll call it off. Now, shall we put it to a vote?"

Despite their obvious misgivings, the decision was unanimous in favor of the plan, at least up to the point of traveling to Medellín and checking into it first-hand. None of the SFX team readily believed that Pablo Escobar was back among the living, but a cool two million dollars plus expenses made the tale worth checking out.

And stranger things had happened, after all.

The Third Reich's Nazis were a case in point. Aside from some ten thousand welcomed into the postwar United States as valued "friends" who labored on behalf of NASA and the CIA, others had scattered farther south, rebuilding lives in South America. No less than four skulls were "identified" as the remains of Adolf Hitler's second-in-command and private secretary, Martin Bormann, between 1945 and '68, while classified reports had him alive and well in Argentina, dreaming of a Fourth Reich that he would command himself. Auschwitz "Angel of Death" Josef Mengele was another monster who refused to stay buried, his death reported time and time again before war's end and 1992, when DNA testing finally confirmed that he'd drowned while swimming at a beach resort in Paraguay.

Hell, as recently as 2019 British journalists had published "overwhelming evidence" that Hitler himself faked suicide in 1945, escaping from Berlin and living to a ripe old age in Argentina.

And if their trip to Medellín turned out to be in vain, at least it would have been a profitable waste of time.

Assuming all of them returned alive.

When the other members of the SFX ensemble had gone home to pack for Medellín, the Mahoney brothers sat together, sipping Bushmills Black Bush Irish Whiskey neat. The Old Bushmills Distillery had been producing first-class liquor in County Antrim, Northern Ireland since 1608, and in Grant Mahoney's opinion it never failed to hit the spot.

"You buy this story?" Blake inquired, as he refilled his glass.

"I'm not buying anything," Grant said. "We're selling services, remember?"

"I get it. But this has a certain smell about it, don't you think?"

"The cartels always do. We've butted heads with them before."

"I'm all for that, don't get me wrong. Take down some bad hombres, light up a lab or two. But chasing ghosts, bro? Seriously?"

"Preston isn't claiming that Don Pablo's back," Grant said. "And you can bet that his director isn't either. But if *anyone* is trying to resuscitate the Medellín Cartel, it's worth a look—particularly if it puts us two mill in the black."

The Medellín Cartel, the brainchild of Escobar brothers Pablo and Ricardo, backed by half a dozen scumbag partners and a small army of ruthless soldiers, had dominated cocaine traffic entering the States from 1976 to '93, supported by high-ranking Colombian politicians and alleged lawmen. At one point, when world opinion forced Don Pablo to accept a prison term in lieu of extradition to America, the men in charge of Bogotá allowed their benefactor to construct his own luxurious prison—dubbed *La Catedral*, "The Cathedral"—where he'd enjoyed gourmet meals, played soccer with the troops who doubled as his guards, soaked in a hot tub or chilled out beneath a manmade waterfall, and watched his family's mini-palace through a telescope. When even that phony captivity began to wear on him, Pablo "escaped" and spent what were presumed to be his last years on the run, pursuing a scorched-earth police of narcoterrorism that included car-bombings, murdering half the judges on Colombia's Supreme Court, slaughtering scores of political opponents and media critics, while blasting commercial airliners out of the sky.

Even former covert allies welcomed his death—or some said suicide—in 1993, but had it all just been another game of smoke and mirrors?

If he had somehow faked his death and had returned now, even in his early seventies, the man who'd once supplied an estimated 85 percent of all cocaine snorted or mainlined in the USA still posed a threat. The bulk of his accumulated fortune—estimated at $30 million ten years before his final shootout—remained unaccounted for. By the time of his reputed death, it might have tripled or quadrupled that, hidden in helpful banks around the globe. No one had thought Pablo was joking back in 1983, when he'd offered to pay off Colombia's $10 billion national debt in exchange for blanket immunity, and that cash hadn't simply disappeared.

Since Escobar's reputed death, his most persistent rivals—based in Cali, 270 miles south of Medellín in the Valle del Cauca department—had been driven out of business, into prison cells or graves, via collaboration of the DEA and various Colombian officials finally disgusted by their homeland's evil reputation. That denouement brought Mexico's several cartels to the fore and ignited a free-for-all south of the border that might never end.

"How far do we trust this contact Preston's lined us up with?" Blake inquired.

"About as far as I can throw the U.S. embassy in Bogotá with one hand tied behind my back," Grant said. "Keeping the DEA at arm's length, we still have to watch out for the CIA, the National Police and damn near anybody else that you can think off. We've agreed to meet him, check him out, but we're not climbing into bed with anyone down there."

"And something else to think about," Blake said. Before Grant had a chance to ask, his brother forged ahead. "This 'ghost' or whatever he is sounds like he's stepping on a lot of toes, and that won't be restricted to Colombia. Offhand, I could name ten or twenty Mexican godfathers who would hate to see Don Pablo make a comeback. Ditto for the Santa Cruz Cartel out of Bolivia."

"No chance that we'll run short of targets then, I guess," Grant said.

"With that in mind..." Blake poured his shot glass full again and tossed it off, then rose to leave. "I'll see you bright and early, then. My go bag's ready, but I need some beauty sleep."

Grant smiled, toasted his younger sibling. Smiled and said, "So, how long did you plan on sleeping in?"

4

José María Córdova International Airport, Medellín

The SFX team was arriving piecemeal, each member prepared beforehand with multiple passports in various names and purported homelands, all with cover stories that should pass inspection unless special scrutiny by experts was applied.

José María Córdova, opened for service in 1985, is Colombia's second-largest airport after El Dorado International in Bogotá, moving more than eight million passengers yearly. Its opening replaced aging Medellín International, offering flights throughout the Western Hemisphere plus regular service to Spain. It stands in the city of Rionegro, twelve miles southeast of Medellín, ranking as the most important airport in the Antioquia Department and in western Colombia, acting as a major hub for Avianca Airlines and its low-cost competitor, Viva Colombia.

Blake Mahoney and Nat Karpin were the only SFX team members flying in together. Natalie had called it drawing the short straw. Their cover cast them as a loving but unmarried couple on vacation, although why they would have chosen Medellín was anybody's guess. In flight they kept their voices down, the only way they could present a vestige of a romantic façade.

"I don't remember how long we've been dating," Blake remarked when they were on final approach.

"Which goes to prove we never were," Natalie said.

"Stuck up much?"

"Call it 'confident'," she answered back.

They'd toasted one another with champagne soon after takeoff, but Natalie had not asked for a refill when the flight attendant came around the second time. She didn't dislike Blake, per se—and had the highest of respect for his ability in action—but the lovey-dovey act rubbed hard against her grain, particularly when she never planned on seeing any of the airline's passengers again.

Still pushing it, Blake said, "I wonder if they'll put us in the honeymooner's suite?"

"Don't count of it," she said. "For one thing, we're not married. For another, someone might get you mixed up with Jackie Gleason, but they'll never think I look a bit like Audrey Meadows."

"Bam, pow, Alice! To the moon!"

"I'd like to see you try it."

"Well…"

"That's what I thought."

"How did your brother pick out our hotel?"

"Location, I suppose. Or maybe he just liked the name."

"Click Clack? What were they thinking? Why not Honk-Honk or Gesundheit?"

"You could always ask the manager."

"Not worth my time."

"Do you want to watch a movie then, and cuddle?"

"Do you want to make it off the plane without a stretcher."

"Ouch!" Blake made a face. "That hurts."

"Count on it. If you get carried away, you'll get carried away."

"I'd like to meet you in the cage sometime," he said, only half teasing her.

"I doubt that."

Finally, they touched down without incident on the airport's solitary asphalt runway, just a tad under twelve thousand feet in length. Jose Maria Airport didn't look like much compared to LAX or JFK, O'Hare or Hartsfield-Jackson in Atlanta, either from the air or after they were on the ground. Nat had to take a moment and remind herself that it served sixteen international airlines plus three domestic and four more hauling cargo. Eight million passengers per year was roughly one-sixth of the country's total population, even more impressive when she factored in that many of those forty-eight-odd million natives spent their lives without a car, much less flying the friendly skies.

Deplaning, Blake and Natalie walked through a warm and misty rain to reach the terminal, still caught up in the "modernizing" process that would ultimately offer travelers flight information via digital displays, high-tech communication, passenger arrival lounges with shopping, plus health services and state-of-the-art security systems. Even so, it was a work in progress, tarps and noisy workmen scattered all around.

Their papers were in order, thanks to SFX retainers, but it hardly mattered. A bored-looking Passport Control officer barely glanced at their documents, stamped them as if in a daydream, and waved them on through. No one in Customs seemed to even think about examining their bags.

Colombia's main smuggling problem, after all, was drugs departing from the country for points north and east, not foreign travelers who might arrive with loads of cash or bearer bonds. As far as weapons went, there were enough in circulation to outfit a revolution or suppress one, law enforcement and the military not included.

They had a car reserved with Hertz and once again experienced no trouble beyond showing drivers' licenses, signing the rental contract and insurance forms that would relieve them of responsibility should something happen to their ride—a possibility they'd factored in as fifty-fifty with their present job in mind.

Some *Medellinense* call their hometown "City of Eternal Spring" or "City of the Flowers," and those nicknames seemed to fit as Blake and Nat followed a road map to their lodging in the suburb known as El Poblado, but this wasn't a first glimpse of Medellín for either of them. Both had seen the city's reeking slums up close and knew that life was cheap here, easily extinguished on a whim.

With any luck they'd live to make it home again.

If not, they didn't plan on checking out alone.

El Dorado International Airport, Bogotá

Avoiding any telltale patterns of behavior was essential for an undercover mission, the first thing any operative thought of on arrival at a destination where he or she stood a decent chance of being killed.

With that in mind, Reg Hardy had not flow directly into Medellín from San Diego International Airport, but rather stopped in Bogotá with a connecting with an Avianca flight between the nation's capital and Antioquia. He'd traveled light, one midsize carryon, trusting that any items he required upon arrival, to protect himself and do his job, would be supplied by SFX's network of accommodating contractors.

Of course, that didn't mean Hardy could trust the locals. Broken promises and back-stabbing graced back to Genesis, when Cain slew brother Abel out of peevish jealousy and got off easy with eviction from Eden. SFX should have an edge of sorts, working on contract for the DEA, but that agency traced its roots to Prohibition in the 1920s, when its agents earned such paltry salaries that very few of them turned out to be "untouchable" where payoffs were concerned.

Granted, the modern DEA was cleaner, overall, and well-funded by U.S. taxpayers to the tune of $3.1 billion yearly, but its problems still made headlines with fair regularity. Its "special" agents had an odd propensity for losing their sidearms in supermarkets, bars, on top of vehicles—and in a men's room at Denver International Airport after its owner had cleared check-in security. Even more embarrassing, a DEA man demonstrating "firearms safety" to grade-schoolers in Florida literally shot himself in the foot, then sued his employer (and lost) when a videotape of the incident leaked to network news outlets.

Beyond such casually clumsiness—and one ludicrous attempt to ban infant pacifiers as "drug paraphernalia"— the DEA had lost various damage suits in federal court, one filed by an innocent man it kept caged for five days without food or water; another by a woman whom a male agent impersonated on Facebook, cyber-stalking the victim and her children; yet another by the parents of a fourteen-year-old boy killed "by mistake." Beyond that, rampant corruption was predictably inevitable: $20 million confiscated dollars missing in one case alone, an agent jailed for pocketing $700,000 during a drug sting.

So, would Reg Hardy trust the government to see him in and out of Medellín alive?

Not even close.

His cover for the mission was that of a wildlife photographer, altered from make-believe big-game hunter on his visa since Colombian lawmakers had banned "sport" hunting in 2019. Today, the country boasted more biodiversity per square mile than any other nation on Earth and ranked as a top destination for eco-tourism. Ostensibly, Hardy hoped to photograph jaguars and jaguarundis, ocelots, pumas and spectacled bears, but in fact the only animals he planned on studying were lowlife *narcotrafficantes*.

And one reputed walking dead man in particular.

He didn't buy the tale of Pablo Escobar pulling a Lazarus routine, but he'd agreed with the Mahoney brothers that if somebody was trying to impersonate the late King of Cocaine, the case deserved further examination. And if DEA headquarters claimed its hands were tangled in Colombian red tape, why shouldn't SFX cash in.

Hardy lived simply for the most part, but two hundred grand would tide him over nicely while he handled independent operations on his own. For starters, it would help support his anti-poaching campaigns overseas, perhaps expanding into western India, where Maharashtra Forest Minister Patangrao Kadam had ruled that injuring or killing tiger poachers was no longer seen as criminal.

About bloody time, too, thought Hardy.

Let the human predators try living in a constant state of fear, knowing their lives were forfeit every time they set foot in the field to prey on nature's "lesser" species in the name of superstition or "tradition." It was time for idiots around the world to learn and understand that powdered rhino horn or tigers' penis would not boost some E.D. victim's potency in bed, that fluids drawn from bears' livers had no impact on kidney failure, and that "trophy" heads mounted on walls were unconnected to the killers' self-styled manhood.

Never mind that now, he thought, and focused on the job at hand, standing in line for his connecting Avianca flight to Medellín. Whatever happened next, Hardy knew he could trust the other members of the SFX team to perform their tasks professionally and efficiently.

He simply wasn't sure if that would be enough to get them home alive.

José María Córdova International Airport

Stan Dartnell missed glimpsing Blake Mahoney and Nat Karpin on arrival, not that he would have acknowledged seeing them in any case. His flight's arrival followed theirs by ninety minutes and they should have been long gone before he cleared Passport Control.

His car was booked through National and he signed the necessary forms, then passed out through glass sliding doors to find it waiting in the nearby parking lot. A map came with the ride, and he consulted it, although he had already memorized the shortest route to El Poblado and the curiously named Click Clack Hotel. He couldn't say who christened the hotel or why, but it was mirrored by another one in Bogotá, which made it an abbreviated chain of sorts. Each room featured a flatscreen television, en suite bathroom, and the upper rooms facing on Calle 10B boasted balconies. His distance from the airport to his lodging came to 1.7 miles.

He was expected to check in under the name on his passport—"Allan Delayne"—and wait until he heard from Grant Mahoney via in-house telephone. From there, the SFX team members would convene to plot their strategy for reaching out to DEA man Preston Chandler's local asset for a briefing on the crazy situation as it stood.

Chandler had named his contact as Camilo Román, age twenty-six, native to Medellín. He had not volunteered to serve the DEA, precisely. Rather, if they could take Chandler at his word, Román had been arrested at Miami International Airport, while smuggling two keys of cocaine in the false bottom of his suitcase. When confronted with the choice of rolling over on his *jefe*, versus ten to fifteen years in prison with the reputation of a loser who had cost the syndicate some sixty thousand dollars, which immediately pinned a bullseye on his back, Román had flipped without a second thought to spare himself. The flake had been returned to him for passage of the pipeline, while a sealed indictment coupled with a signed confession etched the deal in stone.

Except it didn't really.

Dartnell knew that mules caught in a sting were prone to shopping anyone they could, but once they got back home the deal could still go up in smoke. Worse yet, as Chandler might himself suspect, Román could just as easily be acting as a double agent now and feeding crap to DEA headquarters while he lured *gringo* agents into an ambush.

Thinking of that reminded Stan of Vegas and the havoc he had wreaked there, operating on his own initiative without consulting the Mahoney brothers. Grant seemed to be onto him but hadn't mentioned it so far, apparently content to let the feuding between Yakuza and Triads run its course, so long as SFX was left out of the mix. Team members were at liberty to spend their free time as they chose, for profit, vengeance or amusement, if their pastimes didn't blow back on the team.

So far, so good. And if it came around to bite Stan on the backside—if one of the Asian syndicates or both got wise to what he'd done, he would accept the consequences, face whatever happened on his own, and leave his four friends strictly out of it.

For some time after quitting SOCOMD, when he shopped his mercenary skills freelance, the concept of a "friend" would have been alien to Stan Dartnell. He'd lost a few before that, during secret missions for his government, and over time had learned to do without companionship that lasted longer than a few hours in some low-rent hotel. Today, with SFX, his life felt more well-rounded, although not precisely balanced—something that he realized would likely never fall within his grasp again.

And he had come to terms with knowing that each mission he accepted could—and someday *would*—turn out to be his last. Dartnell had slain enough men that the act of killing held no further mystery for him.

As for what happened after death…well, he would have to wait and see. No "holy book" that he had ever read convinced him that a given sect possessed the final, irrefutable answer. Just think how many earnest preachers—and how many frauds—had trumpeted the "Second Coming" over time, many selecting not only its date but a specific hour, all proved fools or charlatans when nothing happened but another sunrise on another humdrum day.

Since he had faced that recognition, Dartnell trusted no one other than himself and his comrades at SFX. If that relationship broke down, he could and would fade back into a solitary life, take each day as it came, and see where life took him.

Approaching the Click Clack Hotel, an angular construction with parts of each floor protruding, other sections set back as if in retreat from traffic and pedestrians below, Darnell thought it resembled life itself. You went along from day to day, then turned a corner and were shocked out of your socks.

And when it ended—possibly tonight, maybe tomorrow or the next day—it would likely come as a surprise.

Click Clack Hotel, Medellín

The hotel's lobby was an atrium of sorts, its centerpieces two large trees rooted in concreted planters ringed by benchers of the same material, flanked by seven-foot-tall lamps, the floor inlaid with elaborately patterned bricks. All around, bars and cafés were open to the central area, their entries topped by porch-type roofs, supporting planters filled with ferns, flowers and shrubbery. Above, four stories high, skylights kept out inclement weather while admitting rays of sunlight to the floor below. The rooms without street-facing balconies had inner windows with a clear view of the lobby and its occupants—dining, drinking, or simply passing through. The smells of cooking food and alcoholic drinks came close to overwhelming Grant Mahoney's senses as he signed the hotel's register, using his passport name of "Sheldon Grant," then homed in on a bank of elevators to his left.

As "Grant," he was supposed to be a California software mogul—no Bill Gates, but on the rise—hoping to outsource factory production if he made an advantageous deal. It wasn't much in terms of cover, no appointments booked with local manufacturers, but if his plan worked out, the SFX team wouldn't be in Medellín that long. The Click Clack's staff cared nothing for his errand in the city, if he paid his bill on time and didn't cause any disturbances.

At least none that they knew about.

His suite was large, befitting Sheldon Grant's rising-star status in Silicon Valley, fitted with a king-sized bed and all attendant frills. The en suite bathroom's shower was contained inside a floor-to-ceiling booth constructed out of tinted glass and steel. Beside it stood a waist-high sink surmounted by a large round mirror and a shelf loaded with toiletries by housekeeping. A toilet and bidet, both jet-black like the sink and shower's frame completed the ensemble.

Grant checked his Hublot Classic Fusion watch and saw it was too early for the other members of his team to be checked into the hotel. He phoned down for room service—cuchuco soup to start, chicken tamales, crepes for dessert—with black coffee to wash it down. Within an hour and a half, at most, his cell phone would announce the other SFX members' arrival, bypassing the Click Clack's office switchboard.

Once they had convened, it would be time to reach out for Camilo Román, said to be a local asset of the DEA. If they could track him down, a face-to-face would be arranged.

But first, before they took that risk, another call would

be required, this one to contacts Grant was reasonably certain he could trust—the emphasis on "reasonably," since there were no solid constants in Colombia.

Those contacts would, or should, come through with hardware to facilitate their next series of moves. And failing that...well, it could see their trip to Medellín cut short, awash in blood.

His food arrived. Mahoney dug in with a will and finished it in something close to record time, still managing to savor every bite. That was a skill he'd learned in basic training, followed on through Delta Force, and it had always served him well. He'd never suffered from a case of indigestion in his life, no matter what he ate, how quickly he consumed it, or the circumstances under which he was compelled to dine.

Call that dumb luck or talent. Either way, he didn't feel inclined to look a gift horse in the mouth just now.

The meal would carry him to midnight and beyond, the strong black coffee keeping him awake until his night's work was completed and he found some time to rest, if that were even possible. The less time spent in Medellín, the better he would like it, but if Preston Chandler's story had even the least basis in fact—not resurrection of a dead man, surely, but some plot to make it seem that way—the trip would be extended.

And the task would shift from information gathering to rooting out the problem, causing it to go away.

Too much to hope for?

Optimism rarely entered into Grant Mahoney's feelings, but self-confidence assured him that if a solution could be found, he and his team of crack professionals stood a fair chance of coming out the other side alive.

And failing that, they would unleash such hell on Medellín that the return of Pablo Escobar, in flesh or fantasy, would be the least of problems faced by local law enforcement or the DEA.

5

Bello, Antioquia

Bello lies twelve miles north of downtown Medellín. Its name translates to English as "The Beautiful One," and while that may be true of its topography, it's safe to say that most inhabitants would disagree.

A recent "quality of life" survey found 39 percent of Bello's population trapped in the "low" socioeconomic strata, 36 percent "medium-low," and 20 percent ranked "low-high," whatever that means. Only 0.1 percent rated "medium-high," their homes described euphemistically as "rustic houses located on the sidewalks." In real-life terms, that left some eighteen hundred of the city's 372,000 inhabitants wealthy enough to lord it over the rest and run things their own way.

Bello sprawls over fifty-fife square miles, but even that is deceiving, less than eight square miles rated as urban. It occupies a tilted plain in the Aburrá Valley of the Andes Mountains, the bulk of its production agricultural, including livestock, coffee—and, of course, cocaine.

Gilberto Garavito only cared about the last part. More specifically, he cared about who grew the coca leaves, processed them into paste, and then refined them into powder that that would turn tremendous profits for his *jefe* and himself upon delivery to the United States. In that pursuit, he had allied himself with a demented genius, falling into line with a bizarre plan to revive a martyred icon, still loved and admired in Antioquia by throngs that rivaled those who'd feared and hated him in life.

Sometimes, Gilberto saw himself as the midwife at the rebirth of Pablo Emilio Escobar Gaviria, founding father of the former Medellín Cartel and Colombia's late "King of Cocaine."

Except that now, "late" was a relative description, swiftly fading like a morning mountain mist.

This evening, as dusk fell over Antioquia, Gilberto and a dozen of *el jefe*'s soldiers stood outside a warehouse in the Bello suburb of La Gabriela, fronting on the Medellín River. Inside, a roughly equal number of selected targets were at work packaging kilos of pure *cocaína* for shipment into Panama, from there to the Bahamas, and beyond that island chain to Florida.

Gilberto and his master had decided that the shipment would be theirs, increasing the substantial fortune of their new revived cartel. But first, its present owners must be laid to rest.

"All ready?" Garavito scanned the faces of his twelve *sicarios,* each man in turn nodding agreement that he was prepared to strike and take no prisoners.

Nine of the soldiers carried automatic rifles, mostly Russian AK-47s, although two of them preferred M4 carbines, a shorter, lighter version of the standard U.S. military issue M16A2 assault rifle. The other three held Benelli M4 Super 90 combat shotguns, semiautomatic weapons loaded with eight twelve-gauge buckshot rounds a piece. Aside from shoulder weapons, each carried at least one sidearm, holstered for convenience on their hips or tucked away in armpit rigs.

Gilberto, as their leader in the absence of their resurrect-ed master, had opted for a Belgian-made FN P90 subma-chine gun, futuristic in its compact bullpup design with an integrated reflex sight and fully ambidextrous controls. The SMG weighed 5.7 pounds and measured less than twenty inches overall. Its unique top-mounted magazine held fifty of manufacturer FN Herstal's small-caliber, high-velocity 5.7×28mm ammunition, firing at a full-auto rate of nine hundred rounds per minute, with a muzzle velocity of 2,350 feet per second and an effective range of 220 yards. His backup weapon was a vintage Bren Ten semiautomatic pistol chambered for 10mm Auto rounds developed in the 1980s and still widely praised as one of that era's best pistols, with a muzzle velocity of 1,600 feet per second.

Most of the individuals they would confront inside the warehouse were grunt labor, clad in skimpy underwear to keep them from secreting any drugs about their persons, but Gilberto knew that half a dozen guards, at least, stood ready to defend the plant. With all that had occurred of late, that number might be larger now.

"Remember," he advised his soldiers. "Cause no dam-age to the *llello*. It is worth more than your life or mine. As for the guards and workers, all must die."

More nods around the ring of hard-faced men who stood before him. Satisfied, Gilberto led them toward the back-door of the warehouse, seemingly unguarded, though he'd seen the CCTV cameras mounted above the loading dock.

The door was locked, of course. One of his shotgunners stepped forward, quickly aimed, and fired four breaching rounds into the door's deadbolt and hinges, then stepped back, reloading as the others rushed inside, Gilberto Ga-ravito bringing up the rear.

More gunfire followed rapidly, Gilberto's point man dropping in his tracks while the remainder blasted anything that moved. The slaughter lasted less than ninety seconds, leaving bodies strewn about the open space, its concrete floor and walls painted with crimson jets of blood.

And in the middle of the room, a long table stood undefended now, heaped with kilos of marching powder shrink-wrapped in plastic. Gilberto did a hasty count, came up with fifteen hundred packages, and did the mental math: $45 million wholesale in Miami or New York.

He smiled, knowing his master would be pleased.

Los Colores, Medellín

Raül Sandino stood two inches taller than his average countryman at five foot seven and seemed taller still in his brigadier general's uniform of the Colombian National Police. Twin ten-pointed golden stars adorned his epaulets, each stamped with his homeland's elaborate coat of arms.

An Andean condor surmounted the seal, holding an olive crown in its beak, talons protruding from beneath a scroll bearing the nation's motto: *Libertad y Orden* ("Liberty and Order"). Below the bird and scroll, Colombia's tricolored national flag draped each side of a shield divided into three sections. The topmost has a pomegranate flanked by cornucopias, one spilling gold and silver coins, the other various tropical fruits. In the middle, a spearpoint supported a Phrygian cap. Below, two old-time sailing ships cruised past the Isthmus of Panama, severed from Colombia in 1903.

Besides that finery, Sandino wore a peaked cap bearing yet another Colombian seal, the hat adding two more inches to his height. A dozen medals glittered on his jacket underneath pole-mounted vapor lamps as he approached his audience with Medellín's new man of mystery, alleged by some to be no less than Pablo Escobar reborn.

Sandino had his doubts on that, to say the least, but he had happily accepted a retainer from the man of mystery, a sum sufficient to serve Raül Sandino as a healthy pension when he finally decided to retire. Not that the payment satisfied him absolutely, mind you. If the man he'd come to meet succeeded, Brigadier Sandino stood to wind up in his golden years a billionaire.

Los Colores, in northwestern Medellín, is a suburb located west of Calle 59 and the Quebrada Iguana River. Sandino's limousine stood idling in the driveway of a mini mansion set on manicured grounds, made noonday bright by floodlights mounted underneath the eaves. Two men stood waiting for him on the broad porch as Sandino left the car, both eyeing him impassively, holding their automatic rifles in a rough approximation of port arms.

They looked him over as Sandino reached the porch, apparently perceived no threat, and one of them opened the tall front door, a houseman on the other side, waiting to serve as escort to a library well stocked with books which, if Sandino was a decent judge, had never been perused.

The man who stood before him certainly resembled Pablo Escobar, as far as Brigadier Sandino could recall from photographs published when he—Sandino—was a teenager. He'd never glimpsed the cocaine baron personally, but he'd read Escobar's file and knew that if the drug lord had survived his final showdown with police he should appear significantly older now, a figure in his early seventies. His host tonight seemed to be closer to Sandino's age in fact and smiling as he scrutinized his guest.

"*Hola*," he said in greeting.

"*Buena noches,* Señor…" Sandino faltered, stuck on the selection of a name.

"Please call me Pablo. I believe that friends should be familiar in their private dealings, eh?"

"Of course, Pablo." Somehow, Sandino managed without choking on the name. "*Gracias* for the invitation to your home."

"I hope we shall see much more of each other as our business grows and prospers, Brigadier."

"Raül, please."

"*Si.* But of course." The smile worn by his undead host seemed genuine enough, but in the circumstances, who could say?

The Pablo lookalike, who seemingly defied not only point-blank execution but the normal wear and tear of age, moved toward a wet bar on the library's east wall. "Aguardiente Antioqueño? Rum, perhaps? Tequila? Beer, if you prefer?"

"Antioqueño, *por favor.*"

Sandino's host poured each of them a generous measure of the liquor considered Colombia's national drink, carried the glasses to a central table flanked by leather-covered easy chairs. They sat, Sandino with his cap resting upon his knees, sipping the liquid fire.

The mansion's owner followed suit, then smiled and said, "Let us discuss how we may make each other what the gringos feign to denigrate, dismissing it as 'filthy rich'."

Castilla, Medellín

"*Muéstrame las armas.*" Not a man who wasted time on "please" or "thank you" in a conversation with subordinates, Filipe "El Tigre" Ortiz demanded presentation of the weapons he had come to purchase for his war in Antioquia.

The vendor, a Colombian named Julián Gamboa, bobbed his head and led Ortiz, trailed by his right-hand man, Isidro Buendia, to stand before a table covered by lumpy oilcloth. Drawing the shroud aside, Gamboa gestured toward the military hardware laid out for display.

"As you requested, Señor Tigre. You will find it all in order."

Ortiz studied the lineup, pleased by what he saw, but shunning any outward sign of satisfaction.

The arsenal included ten AKS-74U carbines, folding stock versions of the Russian AK-74 assault rifle, measuring 19.3 inches to the parent weapon's 37.1 inches, thirteen ounces lighter, chambered for the same 5.45×39mm rounds. The carbine's shorter barrel—8.3 inches versus 16.3—reduced muzzle velocity by 145 feet per second and shaved effective range back from 550 yards to 330, but that hardly mattered. Regardless of size, the weapons still fired at a cyclic rate of ten rounds per second, and no one ever mistook the carbine for a long-range sniper's rifle.

Besides the AKs, there were half a dozen shotguns, equally divided between Mossburg 500 pump-actions and Russian-made Saiga 12 semiautomatics, all twelve-gauge, the Saigas fed from detachable box magazines holding ten to thirty rounds apiece.

Gamboa had also provided eighteen pistols, mostly Glocks, although he'd tossed in three Berettas and one outsized Desert Eagle .44 Magnum designed in Israel, manufactured by Saco Defense, an armaments subsidiary of America's General Dynamics Corporation.

Guns aside, a wooden crate set at the table's far end held what looked to be a couple dozen hand grenades, turned out by Instalaza Corporation based in Zaragoza, Spain, marketed worldwide as the Alhambra brand.

The *pièce de résistance* was another Russian-made weapon, an RPG-7. The rocket-propelled grenade launcher was portable, reusable, unguided and shoulder-launched, designed for anti-tank warfare, but it could serve as well against armored trucks, civilian vehicles or buildings. Its optimum effective range was 360 yards, its 40mm rockets wired to self-detonate at one thousand yards if they missed their targets. Six of those lay in a row beside the launcher, each nearly as long, with its propellant charge, as the thirty-seven-inch launcher itself.

"*Bueno*," Ortega said at last, nodding for Isidro Buendia to deliver final payment. While Gamboa counted rumpled bills, El Tigre said, "I take for granted that you speak to no one else of this transaction, eh?"

Gamboa lost count, glanced up at his customer, came close to blanching if that had been possible, given his dark complexion. "No one, sir! Of course not!"

Ortega considered that, finally nodded. Said, "I hope not, since your life and those of everyone you love depend upon your silence."

"*Si*, Señor! I understand completely."

"In which case, you are excused."

Gamboa hastened to depart. Ortega waited until he had cleared the room, then told Buendia, "*Mátalo* and bring the money back. We'll need it, and I wouldn't trust that worm as far as I can piss against the wind."

Buendia nodded, grabbed a pistol from the table, checked its load, and followed their supplier into outer darkness.

Ortiz had obtained more weapons than his crew of fifteen men required, but he preferred having too many, rather than to find himself caught short. A snatch of dialogue from a Clint Eastwood western movie came to mind, a one-armed sheriff's deputy explaining why he carried to revolvers. "I never want it said," the character declaimed, "that I got killed for lack of shooting back."

From Castilla, four miles north of downtown Medellín, El Tigre planned to launch a war. His overlords, commanding Mexico's dominant Guadalajara Cartel, expected positive results with no excuses for failure. The rising threat from one who claimed to be infamous Pablo Escobar reborn—or risen from the depths of Hell where he belonged—must be eliminated if Ortiz planned on returning home again.

Failing at that, El Tigre knew he might as well pick up the Desert Eagle .44 and turn it on himself right now. Death by his own hand would be preferable to the fate his *jefe* would devise for one who let him down on such a grand scale.

Ortiz was not worried about failure in the abstract. So far, he had always taken adequate precautions to avoid it and survive whatever trials he faced. There was no reason he should fail this time, despite the heavy odds arrayed against him. Only one thing truly troubled El Tigre.

He had no clue what it might take to kill a ghost.

Pablo—the real one—was deceased. Ortiz knew that as certainly as he knew that his given middle name, sadly misplaced, was "Angel."

No, there was no walking revenant or zombie to be hunted and destroyed, only a man who had somehow convinced others of his investment with some supernatural authority to warp the rules of time and space. That legend, having taken root already from the slums of Antioquia to Bogotá's exalted halls of government, was his real enemy. How he might slay it, bury it beyond recall, was anybody's guess.

Buendia came back from the warehouse parking lot bearing the heft roll of cash Ortiz had given to Gamboa moments earlier. Ortiz accepted it, pleased to discover that the banknotes were not damp or stained with blood,

"The body?"

"Being taken care of as we speak," Buendia said. "There'll be no trace of him until we're all long gone, if then."

"Bueno. Let us collect the tools, then, and begin to finalize our plans."

Los Colores, Medellín

"Diga me," the man who called himself Don Pablo Escobar instructed. "Tell me."

"*Sí, jefe.*" Gilberto Garavito carefully described his raid against the target he had been assigned in Bello, with a head count of the adversaries executed and a tabulation of how much the captured *cocaína* ought to net when it was moved to buyers in the States.

"No difficulties, then?" his lord and master asked.

"One of our men suffered a minor flesh wound to the leg," said Garavito. "Simón Obregón."

"Yes. I remember him."

"*El doctor* has him now. It's trivial. We should expect a full recovery."

"All good news, then."

"*Sí, jefe.*"

"What about the *Mexicanos*, Gilberto?"

"The Mexicans? Which Mexicans, Señor?"

"*Which* Mexicans? The ones who have invaded Medellín, *amigo*. Why are you not briefing me on their activities?"

Garavito blinked, mouth working like the spastic jaws of a grounded catfish, before he stammered in reply, "*Jefe*, I am afraid…that is to say…."

"I hope you are afraid," his leader interrupted. "It severely disappoints me that I hear from others what I'm paying you to tell me in advance."

"*Disculpas, jefe. Lo siento mucho.*"

"Save your apologies. It's information that I need."

Caught off-balance, clearly terrified of making matters worse, Gilberto hazarded a guess. "Guadalajara, *sí*? I warned you that they would attempt to stop us, Pablo."

"Did you warn me they were here, Gilberto? In my own backyard right now? Did you advise me that they've sent their most respected contractor, with no less than fifteen *sicarios*?"

"El Tigre?"

"*Sí*. The very same."

"I will investigate immediately, *jefe*. That is, if you trust me to continue."

"I insist upon it," his commander answered back. "Rest not until you know their whereabouts, full strength, and any necessary details of their plan. I want them rubbed out. Muerto. Gone as if they never lived at all."

"It shall be done, *jefe*."

"I will not tolerate a second disappointment, Gilberto."

"No, *jefe*. I begin at once."

"And don't return without the information I require of you."

As Garavito hastened from his presence, grateful to be breathing when his night of triumph might have ended with a scream of agony, the man Gilberto knew as Pablo Escobar reborn allowed himself another glass of Aguardiente Antioqueño to enjoy in solitude.

His name, as Garavito must have realized by now, although too awed to challenge the pretense, was not and never had been Pablo Escobar. In fact, he had been christened Jorge Torrenegra thirty-seven years ago and was a distant cousin of the man all Medellín had once hailed as a benefactor and a martyr or reviled as Satan in the flesh. When Escobar went down for good in 1993, Jorge had grown accustomed to his kin remarking on his physical resemblance to the famous relative he'd never met in life.

Life in Colombia offers three prospects for advancement: politics, back-breaking labor, or cocaine. Taking his cue from Escobar, Jorge had picked the latter path. The first two shipments he had personally carried into the United States, risking his life or major prison time, established Torrenegra as a minor player in the *llello* trade. The next few gave him breathing room while he devised a master plan, dropped out of sight to undergo a course of plastic surgery that would enhance his born resemblance to the cocaine king while adding years to Jorge's visage rather than subtracting them, as most patients desired.

His doctor in Cali had been surprised, remarking that Jorge was his first patient who desired to look *older,* while creating scars—and most specific scars, at that—rather than stripping them away. That observation, casual at first, had sealed the surgeon's fate and Torrenegra had removed his file, complete with its before-and-after photographs, erasing any link between himself and the late doctor, said to be the victim of a bungled office robbery.

Today, Torrenegra had become a living legend—or a dead one, resurrected by some means never explained—to people ranging from Colombia to Mexico and farther north. None knew precisely what to make of him, the legend he had spun around himself, but Torrenegra had elicited responses from old friends, whatever enemies his distant cousin had not slain, from politicians and police. Victory was within his grasp, but he could still lose everything through one egregious mistake.

The man who would be king finished his drink, prepared to make an early night of it and sleep alone for once. He had no wife, no regular lover, no living relatives who might have recognized him after his expensive transformation. At present, it was safest for him to remain a solitary man, immune to physical distractions and emotional entanglements.

There would be time enough to build a family, if he were so inclined, when he was well and truly recognized as king of all that he surveyed.

Until then, nothing else mattered.

And if he failed, at last…well, nothing mattered then, either, except to write his name in history, with blood-red letters ten feet tall.

6

Asomadera Park, Medellín

"You think he'll show?" asked Blake Mahoney.

"Fingers crossed," his brother Grant replied. "We're pretty much dead in the water without him."

"I have to say that Chandler left me feeling hinky."

"I'd agree, but he needs information from us. No percentage in it for him, dicking us around."

"Unless somebody farther up the ladder has a score to settle we don't know about."

"We've never had a beef with DEA before," Grant said. "If they were gunning for us, why not make a move at home, instead of flying us down here?"

"Deniability, for one thing," Blake suggested. "Some of them are just damned devious, besides."

"We'll take it slow and easy, bro. And don't forget we're covered."

For triangular converging fire, in fact, with Hardy, Karpin and Dartnell on station, watching out for any traps, ready to make their move if anything smelled rotten.

Anything beyond the usual in Medellín, that was.

The team had stocked up on equipment from a local dealer they'd done business with before, no reason to distrust him other than the fact that he existed in Colombia. The brothers carried Glocks with sound suppressors, while their teammates had more firepower available at need. Grant hoped it wouldn't come to that so quickly, but it always helped to be prepared.

Asomadera Park was one of Medellín's natural treasures, lovingly maintained, some eighty-three green acres wedged between the suburbs of Las Palmas, San Diego and El Salvador. Its crowning glory, Cerro la Asomadera, looms sixteen hundred feet above sea level, ranked with Pan de Azúcar Hill, El Salvador Hill, El Volador Hill, El Picacho Hill, Las Tres Cruces Hill, Nutibara Hill and Santo Domingo Hill as one of Medellín's "guardian" or "tutelary" hills offering panoramic views of Antioquia's capital city.

After nightfall, it was also a primary "cruising" site for members of the gay community, on par with Central Park in New York City or San Francisco's Golden Gate Park. No lonely men had neared the two Mahoney brothers at their hilltop table yet, nor had they glimpsed the contact Preston Chandler had arranged from stateside.

And Camilo Román, by Grant's watch, was running late. Not much, so far, but seven minutes in the heart of Medellín could be a lifetime and then some.

Grant made a quick radio check with the SFX team's other members, strategically posted around Asomadera Hill. Dartnell and Hardy had no action to report, but Natalie announced a solitary stroller moving toward the hilltop, acting vaguely nervous.

"Physical description?" Grant inquired.

"He looks enough like Román's photograph to pass," she answered back. "Which isn't saying much. He could be any third or fourth guy on the street in Medellín."

"You have him covered, Number Two?"

Grant's query that time went to Hardy, waiting with his

sniper's rifle to unload on any threat that came their way.

"I've got him now," the Brit came back. "It *could* be him, but I'd agree it's hard to say."

Especially with someone running wild and claiming to be Pablo Escobar, Grant thought. And said to all his watchers, "Fair enough. Just cover him and see what happens next."

Blake shifted on his concrete bench and eased a hand inside his lightweight windbreaker, ready with his pistol if the wrong guy showed his face or Camilo Román had some trick up his sleeve.

"I've got him," Blake announced.

Grant turned, followed his younger sibling's gaze, and saw a man approaching. He stood five foot six or seven, seeming smaller from the way his shoulders slumped. Unruly hair—combed better in the photo they'd received from Preston Chandler back in San Diego—crowned an oval face, dark halfmoons visible beneath the twitchy eyes.

"From here, I can't tell if he's high or just about to blow a gasket," Blake observed.

"Could be the jumpy sort," Grant said, "with Chandler squeezing him to give up Pablo two-point-oh."

"Or maybe setting us up," Blake suggested. "Worried about getting caught up in the crossfire."

"If it breaks that way, we'll make sure that he does."

"Damn straight."

The man approaching them now wore a denim jacket, jeans to match, and running shoes that had seen better days. His hands were thrust into the jacket's pockets, out of sight, until Grant signaled him to stop and made a show of spreading out his own hands, empty for inspection. Román—there could be no doubt as to his I.D. now—complied, turning the pockets inside-out to show he'd left no weapons stashed in either one of them.

"Give us a spin," Blake said, and made spun his left hand

in a circle, while his right still gripped the hidden Glock.

Again, Camilo Román followed orders, hoisting up his jacket's hem as he revolved, showing that nothing had been clipped onto his belt or tucked beneath it.

"Okay," Grant said. "Have a seat. Let's talk."

Before he sat down on the cold, hard bench, Román surveyed the hilltop park surrounding him and the two gringos he had been assigned to meet.

"Expecting company?" the slightly older, somewhat taller of them asked.

"Hoping for none," Román replied.

"No sweat," the other said. He looked enough like his companion that they might have been related somehow. "We've had people tracking you. You're clean, unless you want to tell us something off the top. Maybe a homer stitched into your clothes? A drone somewhere up high?"

"Nothing," said the Colombian. "I have no wish to be here, much less broadcast the event."

"But here you are," the first gringo to speak replied. Román fixed him in mind as Number One and did not bother asking for a name.

"My *manipulador*—how you say it, 'handler'—gave me no choice in the matter."

"And his name would be...?" asked Number Two.

"You know his name."

"So, humor me."

"He introduced himself to me as Preston Chandler. Whether that's his name in fact, I cannot say."

"That would have happened when the DEA arrested you for smuggling coke into the States," said Number One.

"*Sí.*" Román saw no point in evading what they must have known already.

"And you cut a deal to save yourself," said Number Two.

"Just as you say."

Still Number Two: "Which brings us to this fairy tale about the zombie, Pablo Escobar."

"I know these zombies from *The Walking Dead,* eh? We have HBO in Medellín. Pablo is not some wandering *cadáver,* pieces falling off, lurching about and snarling like an animal."

"You've seen him, then?" asked Number One.

"One time, briefly," Román allowed. "Emerging from a limousine downtown and entering the Woka Lounge downtown, on Calle 38. I recognized him clearly from no more than twenty feet away, with his *sicarios.*"

"You knew him earlier, when he was still alive?" asked Number One. "What were you back then, five or six years old?"

"Seven," Román corrected him. "But seeing Don Pablo in those days was something you don't forget."

"And how'd he look this time?" asked Number Two. "We're calculating that if this isn't a load of crap, he must be going on seventy-eight by now."

Román could only shrug at that. "The Pablo Escobar I saw may have been half that age, perhaps a little more."

"Somebody's had him in suspended animation then, and just now brought him back?" asked Number One. "Is that the theory?"

"I have no *teoría,*" Román said. "I can only tell you what I've seen and what is said about him on the streets."

"So, fill us in on that." Again, from Number One.

"First, that his riches are beyond compare to those of any president or potentate. Like many *narcotrafficantes,* he was known to dabble in the ways of *brujería*—what you in *el norte* call witchcraft, *magia negra*—and he dealt with many scientists related to his business, some of them with interests beyond processing *llello.*"

"Such as?" Number Two inquired.

"When Nazi scientists escaped from *Alemania* after

the last World War, they did not all wind up in the United States, building your rockets to the moon. More found their way to South America and carried on their scientific research into life and death."

"Uh-huh." The skepticism radiated vibrantly from Number Two.

"You doubt me?" Román challenged him. "Are you familiar with the refugees in Chile at Colonia Dignidad? Each year they celebrate the Führer's birthday with a beauty pageant for the choicest Aryan women among them. Scandal forced them underground in 1991, two years before Pablo was said to have been killed. In fact, only the name changed. It is called Villa Baviera today—'Bavaria' in English—and it's said the same experiments go on with twins and so forth. Josef Mengele was known to visit there and join in certain operations, while he ran a clinic of his own in Paraguay, protected by the Alfredo Stroessner's government."

"You claim that Nazis found a way to bring back Pablo Escobar after the Search Bloc blew his brains out here in Medellín?" asked Number One.

"You asked for theories. That is one of them. Since I did not participate, I cannot say."

"Why would a bunch of German psychos on the run help Escobar?" asked Number Two.

"Perhaps because he was one of the richest men on Earth," Román suggested, "who could bankroll their insanity for years with a small portion of his earnings from your addicts in America."

"All right," said Number One. "Enough about how Pablo or whoever might have pulled it off. We need to know two things from you. First, what has he been up to lately? Second, where can we clap eyes on him right now?"

"The first part is no mystery," Camilo Román said. "Street whispers, what you call the grapevine, follow him as if he were a pop star like Shakira or Andrés Cabas. Each day and night he makes more progress toward reviving his cartel, expanding it beyond the wildest dreams of his former heyday."

"We'll need details," said Number Two.

"I'll tell you what I can but have no proof for much of it beyond hearsay and rumor. As to finding him…" Roman's voice trailed away.

"Go on," said Number One.

"It all depends on how badly you wish to die."

Reg Hardy scanned the park with the PSO-1M2 4×24 telescopic sight affixed to his OTs-03 SVU sniper rifle. No one was encroaching on the three-man meeting underway down range, although a nervous-looking pair of young men was apparently negotiating terms for sex a hundred yards southwest of where the SFX team's CEO and Veep were huddled with the DEA asset they'd come to meet.

Hardy confirmed as best he could that the prospective lovers were not putting on an act as cover for a sneak attack and left them to it, going for another sweep around his comrades and their contact.

Both his rifle and its special sight were Russian made, a nod toward plausible deniability if the weapon was lost or captured before the SFX commandos finished up their work in Medellín. The rifle's "SVU" designation stood for *Snájperskaja Vintóvka Ukoróčennaja* ("sniper rifle shortened"), distinguishing its bullpup configuration from progenitor, the venerable Dragunov SVD in used by Russian forces between 1968 and 2013, still carried by marksmen in forty-odd armies worldwide.

The transition to bullpup design shaved 1.6 pounds from the parent weapon's weight and shortened it by fourteen inches. Recoil was reduced from the original by adding a muzzle brake to absorb 40 percent of the SVU's energy on firing, further eased by an elastic butt stock with lamellar spring non-rigidly attached to the receiver. Otherwise, it fired the same 7.62×54mmR cartridges that fed the Dragunov, loaded in detachable box magazines holding ten to thirty rounds. The SVU's shorter barrel reduced muzzle velocity from 2,723 feet per second to 2,645, but that scarcely mattered to targets on the receiving end of semiautomatic fire. The SVU also came with an integral flash hider and a bayonet lug, though Hardy couldn't picture any long-range shooter charging over open ground, wielding the relatively stubby Russian blade in hand-to-hand combat.

With no action on the hilltop, Hardy checked on Stan Dartnell and Natalie Karpin. He didn't use his walkie-talkie, saving that for an emergency, but picked out each teammate in turn using his rifle's scope, each still in the position he or she had staked out on arrival at Asomadera Park.

Dartnell was hidden underneath a hedge of marmalade bushes, neatly pruned against the perennial evergreens' constant drive to spread. Karpin was wedged into the lower branches of an encenillo tree, some twenty feet above ground level. Both were armed with AK-9 compact assault rifles, chambered in 9×39mm, equipped with sound suppressors, folding stocks and laser sights. The weapons had an effective range of 433 yards and a full-auto cyclic fire rate of 750 rounds per minute.

Both SFX teammates also carried Glock sidearms, as did Hardy and the two Mahoney brothers, just in case the action moved up close and personal. If it came closer still, they also were equipped with fighting knives, Hardy's personal choice being the Fairbairn–Sykes model he'd mastered while serving with the SAS.

Ideally, none of them would fire a shot tonight. The

meeting with their DEA contact would go as planned, fresh information sending them farther along the trail toward whoever was claiming to be the wraith of Pablo Escobar back home on Earth.

Between his time with SAS and taking to the field with conservation officers from Africa to Southeast Asia, Hardy had seen a fair share of the planet he inhabited, while spending little time at home on England's "green and pleasant land." His last significant deployments while in uniform had been "Operation Jubilee" in May 2012 and "Operation Shader," executed fifteen months later.

The first paired SAS commandos with warriors of the U.S. Naval Special Warfare Development Group (DEV-GRU) to rescue four aid workers kidnapped by bandits and held in in the Koh-e-Laram forest of northeastern Afghanistan's Badakhshan Province, wedged between Tajikistan and northern Pakistan. The hostages—two Afghans, one Brit and one Kenyan—were reportedly stashed in two separate caves, but that intel had proved to be wrong. When DEVGRU troops hit the first site, arriving in a Blackhawk helicopter, they'd killed seven bandits but found no prisoners. Meanwhile, Hardy's squad, in a second Blackhawk, rescued all four prisoners and finished off four kidnappers. None of the grateful prisoners or their rescuers suffered any injuries.

"Operation Shader," launched in August 2014, was another rescue mission, helping Yazidi refugees besieged by Muslim fanatics from the Islamic State of Iraq and the Levant (ISIL) in its genocidal campaign to rid Iraq and its neighboring nations of non-Islamic influences. That effort lit the fuse for a protracted ground war against ISIL that continued to the present day, producing an official estimate of 4,023 dead—all but ten of them ISIL—plus one journalist missing and presumed slain. British Prime Minister David

Cameron had seized the spotlight, vowing that ISIL would "be squeezed out of existence," but so far that bluster had produced no more success than his other media statements before a referendum sent him packing in 2016.

By that time, Hardy had been circulating as a free agent abroad and he preferred it that way, while regretting nothing that he'd done in service to the Union Jack. He wasn't wild about this visit to Colombia, chasing a phantom, but the price was right.

And with a bit of luck, he might just make it out alive.

"That's all of it?" asked Grant Mahoney, eyes raised toward Camilo Román from his notebook, lying open on the concrete picnic table. Its water-soluble pages were nearly translucent, thinner than normal tissue paper, and could be destroyed in seconds flat by placing them inside a subject's mouth.

The days of spies and bookies scribbling notes on flash paper, which could be set alight but smothered and retrieved if raiders closed in fast enough, had gone the way of whalebone corsets and transistor radios.

Mahoney watched Román for any clue that he had lied during their interview or might be holding vital information back. The guy was none too happy to be speaking with them, but he'd flashed no tells that indicated he was lying, struck no body language postures that suggested he'd approached their meeting with intention to deceive.

But if Román believed what he had told them...well, so what?

Belief was easy, the foundation of all known religions throughout history, leaders of most declaring theirs to be the "only truth." That wouldn't wash, of course, since every creed had zealots on its side, committed without question to what finally came down to nothing more than group opinion. If belief alone made something "true," then simple logic proved that *all* religions, all political assertions must be accurate.

And that, of course, negated all of them across the board.

"There's nothing else," Román replied to Grant's inquiry.

"How long has it been since you confirmed these various addresses?" Grant pressed his informant.

"Most within a week or two," Román answered. "As for the public sightings, accurate or not, the clubs and restaurants are still in business. You can question managers and staff yourselves."

"We just might do that," Blake Mahoney said, frowning at Román, but both brothers knew that kind of legwork would be wasting time. What did it matter if a bartender or bouncer thought he had seen Pablo Escobar alive and well last week, last month?

It did the SFX team no concrete good at all.

To prove the case, the fraud, whatever, *they* would have to see the man posing as Escobar, devise some way to separate him from his street soldiers, and put hard questions to him.

Find out what in Hell was really going on.

And once they had that information in their hands, the task remained twofold.

First, report to Preston Chandler at the DEA.

Second, eliminate the problem in a way that satisfied their client, whether that meant setting up a string to land the Escobar impersonator behind bars or go all out and put him in the ground.

Grant had no preference on that score, though his team was not equipped for extradition operations from a nation with a history as troubled as Colombia's. If Chandler sought to travel that route, he would have to get the proper paperwork in order, plus sufficient local backup, through negotiations with Colombia's attorney general and perhaps with the incumbent president himself. Diplomacy did not fall under SFX's purview, and Mahoney had no taste for it.

He wasn't a committee man, aside from serving as his brainchild's CEO, and never hoped to be. Negotiation, in Grant's view, most often closed the door on useful action and allowed problems to fester, sometimes lapsing from benign into lethal malignancy.

"May I go now?" Camilo Román asked, addressing neither one of his interrogators personally.

Grant and Blake Mahoney shared a glance, the Grant replied, "We need to stay in touch. The cell phone where we reached you is in service all the time?"

Román nodded. Answered, "I need it for *mi ocupación.*"

His occupation, as Grant knew, was running drugs and double-dealing his competitors, suppliers, damned near anyone at all to law enforcement if it offered Román an advantage for himself. By definition he could not be trusted, but so far he was their only source of information on the job they had accepted from the DEA. That meant they had to tolerate him to a point, but if he crossed a line that jeopardized Mahoney's team, the weasel would be going out of business permanently.

And he wouldn't be returning from grave to strut his stuff in Medellín.

"All right," Grant said. "But if we call, you answer, right? No ducking us until were out of here. If you make us come looking for you, you won't like how it goes down."

"*Sí, sí.* I understand."

Rising in haste, their so-called asset scuttled off into the night.

7

Las Penitas, Medellín

The first target selected from Camilo Román's short list was supposed to be a *llello* cutting plant off Calle 4366 in the city's Thirteenth District, where murders happened with a numbing frequency, most winding up unsolved or being "cleared" by framing some someone from the city's glut of homeless down-and-outs.

That came as no surprise, considering the Medellín Police Department's record of involvement with narcotics traffickers spanning the past four decades, guarding cocaine shipments, loading transport planes, and sometimes serving as hired guns. Barely a year had passed since lawless cops themselves had been accused of ransom kidnappings and operating citywide extortion rackets.

If the SFX team's first raid fell apart, they could expect no help from anybody carrying a badge.

They took three rental cars, Natalie Karpin bringing up the rear of their little parade alone—the way she liked to operate whenever possible. All carried AK-9 assault rifles and Glocks, coupling deniability of provable American involvement with emergency coordination of their weapons' calibers and magazines. Reg Hardy doubled up with his

SVU sniper's rifle, under orders to hang back and cover all approaches to the target while remaining primed to wade in closer if the others needed backup.

If Román had given them the straight dope—pun intended—their first move would be against a lab that occupied the second story of an old commercial building, with a laundromat downstairs. Locals with pocket change to spare could wash their clothes around the clock, served by a sleepy clerk if anything went wrong with one of the machines. The clerk also controlled a panic button that would warn the crew upstairs of an impending raid—not that they'd ever suffered one, considering the regular *mordida*—"bite," or bribe—they shelled out to keep lawmen blind and dumb.

Tough luck for "Pablo" or whoever ran the operation, though.

Tonight's drop-ins weren't cops, nor were they on the cartel's pad.

The team had planned their strike in conference at the Click Clack Hotel, plotting approaches and escape routes on a detailed map of Medellín. They would move in from three sides, the Mahoney brothers, Stan Dartnell and Natalie closing on foot, boxing the target in, while Hardy covered them from the rooftop of a four-story office building that had witnessed better days. Their first move was to take the laundromat and its watchman by storm—Natalie's task— before they swarmed upstairs and hit the cutting plant.

If they succeeded, and if none of them were killed or badly wounded, step one of their plan should cost the re-born Medellín Cartel a tidy bundle at the going wholesale rate for product sold Stateside. At thirty grand per kilo, losses mounted quickly and were bound to prompt a furi-ous reaction from the man in charge, whoever he might be.

No parting conversation passed between them, each

driver proceeding to the point that he or she had been assigned. Their cars—no flashy rides among them to arouse neighborhood thieves or gabbing busybodies—nestled into parking slots well separated from each other, boxing in the block, and long coats covered weapons that might well have startled passersby, even in Las Penitas. Extra magazines and frag grenades made pockets droop with extra weight but would not slow them down.

It was supposed to be a simple in and out, blitzing the plant, its guards, and anybody else who tried to stop them going in or out. That said, misgivings still dogged Grant Mahoney as he parted from his brother, pacing off a half block to the laundromat where he had drawn the short straw, tasked to neutralize the clerk-cum-handyman and lookout for the goons upstairs.

He had a pair of handcuffs for the clerk if that proved feasible, but he expected trouble and wasn't about to let the operation fall apart before his teammates even got upstairs, from sympathy for some cartel employee he had never met and didn't care to know.

The cocaine trade was deadly. Everyone involved in it knew that.

Tonight, Mahoney's team would drive that lesson home.

"This is the place?" Felipe Ortiz asked no one in particular.

"*Sí, jefe*," his driver answered. "Upstairs from the *lavandería*."

El Tigre saw no one inside the laundromat except a clerk behind the register. Binoculars revealed that he was busy gaping at the photos in a nudie magazine, glancing occasionally toward the street beyond windows that needed washing.

Ortiz and five of his men were riding in a black rented Toyota RAV4 SUV. Six more of his *sicarios* were covering the far side of the block, driving a Honda Passport—also rented, also black—to move in from the rear. His last four soldiers, held back in reserve, were parked a block east of the laundromat, in a gray Subaru Forester.

El Tigre keyed his walkie-talkie and addressed the team waiting behind their target, using code on the off chance some taxi driver or punk kid with a ham radio might listen in on their selected frequency.

"Tiger to Raptor. Are you clear?"

"*Claro, jefe.* Ready when you are."

"*Bueno,*" Ortiz answered. "Move in now."

His word would put five men in motion, while their driver lingered with the vehicle, watching for *el policia* or any other threat. Switching his two-way radio to "OFF," El Tigre stepped out of the RAV4's shotgun seat, his wheelman staying put, the others joining him in a tight cluster on the sidewalk. None made any serious attempt to hide their AKS-74U carbines as they crossed the street and closed in on the laundromat some fool had christened Espuma y Burbujas—translated to *Inglés* as "Suds and Bubbles."

"Are they serious?" one of his gunmen asked another.

"*¡Cállate!*" Ortiz snapped at the loose-lipped soldier without glancing back at him.

The triggerman knew better than to offer an apology when he'd been told to shut his mouth.

"First thing through the door," El Tigre told them all, "deal with the *idiota* at the register. Remember that he serves the men upstairs."

His people all knew that, but Ortiz didn't mind stating the obvious to his subordinates, when the alternative was failure capped by death.

Another thirty yards to go, and there was no one on the street worth worrying about so far. A solitary woman was approaching from the opposite direction, westbound, walking with her head down, hands inside the pockets of her knee-length raincoat. Ortiz couldn't judge her looks from that distance, with the poor streetlights that illuminated Las Penitas, and it did not matter anyway.

He wasn't out for sex tonight, but rather blood.

If the attack went well, he and his men could always celebrate its aftermath with *putas* back in their rooms at the Stanza Hotel Medellín. A little something extra for the working girls should line them up as alibis on the off chance that any *policías* turned up later, asking questions.

Killing two birds with a single stone.

But first, to business.

Ortiz jacked a round into his carbine's chamber and his soldiers followed suit, metallic rasping sounds reverberating up and down the street from mostly closed small shops and offices.

"*Prepárate hombres,*" El Tigre cautioned his *sicarios*. "Be ready, men."

He trusted that they would not fail him, even if the night ended with some of them no longer drawing breath. Each soldier knew the risks and the rewards involved in service to the Guadalajara Cartel and accepted both upon applying for the job. Death shadowed every step they took from that point on, and there was no retirement plan for an old age that most of them would never see.

Ortiz pushed through the coin-op laundry's main entrance, leveling his AK at the startled clerk while his men formed a skirmish line behind him. He was on the verge of firing when the woman he had noticed earlier entered, using a doorway on the laundromat's east side, stopped short, and startled him with an extraordinary smile.

"Trouble!" Reg Hardy's voice sounded in Karpin's Bluetooth earpiece. "We've got hostiles moving in."

"Tell me about it," she replied, and flashed the enemy her most engaging smile before the whole plan fell apart.

In front of her, the hit team's point man had begun to turn, his automatic weapon tracking to the right, in Natalie's direction. When she smiled, it must have thrown him off, because he hesitated for a critical split-second, giving her just time enough to raise her AK-9 and slip her index finger through its trigger guard, already taking up the slack.

She fired a three-round burst of 9×39mm from the hip, already breaking toward the laundry's checkout counter, aiming for the guy who'd meant to take her down. It was her turn to be surprised, as he seemed to collapse *before* she opened fire, a move that put him prone on the dingy linoleum, angling for target acquisition as he hit the floor.

Because he'd ducked, Natalie's bullets struck one of the riflemen lined up behind the one who seemed to be their leader, punching him backwards, blood spraying from chest wounds, turning his cry of pain into a gargled gasp.

The other three, still on their feet, were scattering for cover as she reached the counter, barreled through a swinging gate that wouldn't have deterred a six-year-old, and dropped into a fighting crouch.

In front of Natalie, the laundry's clerk was gaping at her, wide-eyed, while he plucked a sawed-off shotgun from its scabbard just below the register. As the other armed in-truders opened fire, raking the counter, blasting through its minimal and doubtless stale display of snacks and candy, he was focusing on Nat—the nearest threat that he could see— pumping a twelve-gauge round into the shotgun's breech.

She didn't give him time to fire, shearing his frightened face off with her second three-round AK burst. The look-out's blood and brains painted the register above him and the floor below, his nearly headless form collapsing into death.

That hadn't been a part of Karpin's plan, although she had

anticipated decking him before he got the chance to warn the *llello* cutting team upstairs, but new arrivals on the scene had sent her previous intentions swirling down the crapper.

It was do-or-die time now.

And Natalie did not intend to be the first one ambulance attendants carried out of Suds and Bubbles in a body bag.

It would have been a fool's game standing up and trading shots with four opponents in the laundromat, particularly when the counter that concealed her had already proved its weakness as a shield. Instead of popping up again, she reached into the left-hand pocket of her raincoat and retrieved one of the frag grenades that their supplier had provided with the AK-9s and Glocks.

She'd added it for an emergency, if one arose.

Her present situation seemed to fit the bill.

Natalie pulled the grenade's safety pin and dropped it, cocked her arm and tossed the fourteen-ounce spherical bomb overhand toward the laundry's main workspace. Spanish was not one of her five fluent languages, but she still recognized a warning shout of *"¡Granada! ¡Cuidado!"*

Whether the "look out" command saved all of them, she couldn't tell from where she lay concealed. The M67's Composition B explosive charge went off like thunder in the laundry, battering around four walls, reverberating from the washers and dryers. She heard glass shattering and someone crying out as if in pain, knowing that she could wait no longer for the necessary follow-up.

Rising, she swept the room with narrowed eyes over her rifle's sights, surprised to find three of the five *sicarios* she had surprised already fleeing toward the street. Two others—one she'd shot, the other clutching at his bloody abdomen where shrapnel lay imbedded—were beyond escaping now.

Nat finished off the screamer and told any members of her team still listening, "I'm on my way upstairs."

Reg Hardy saw three of the hitmen who had barged into the laundromat retreating now, sprinting across the street toward their RAV4 and waiting driver.

He called out to SFX member who might be listening, "Heavies are on the run now, but you heard the racket. Won't be long until the cops start showing up. I'll try to slow them down."

With that, he broke off contact, focusing his rifle's PSO-1M2 scope on the retreating trio, whoever they were. The RAV4's driver revved its engine, dropped it into gear, but waited for his pals to reach the vehicle. Hardy lined up his first mark on the run—tricky, but with the shooter running toward him he wasn't required to lead the target—and triggered his first round of the fight.

Hardy stroked his OTs-03 SVU's trigger, recoil absorbed by its butt stock's internal spring, and sent a 7.62×54mmR projectile buzzing down range at 2,600 feet per second. It drilled the last runner in line, striking with 2,761 foot-pounds of explosive energy, drilling completely through his chest and out his back, gouging the asphalt he had lately crossed. It blew the shooter over backwards, shoulders touching down before his hips or heels, and he was stone-cold dead before he hit the pavement.

That left two, plus one behind the black Toyota's steering wheel. Hardy had no clue who he was firing at, beyond the fact that none of them wore uniforms and all were packing guns when they entered the Suds and Bubble laundromat, confronted there by Natalie Karpin.

They might have killed her then and there, while Hardy watched, but she'd been faster on the draw and wrapped up the engagement with a hand grenade that took her opposition by surprise. Now three of the initial five were down and out, but Hardy didn't like to let the last three slip away.

Both fleeing gunmen who'd survived so far piled into the Toyota's backseat from the driver's side, obscured from view of Hardy's scope, before the wheelman revved his mill and screeched off from a standing start. Hardy swung to his right, trying to fix his sights crosshairs onto a point where he could drill the driver's head, but when he fired, his slug punched through the SUV's roof farther back than he'd intended, likely burrowing into the driver's headrest.

Cursing, Hardy tried again, but by the time his third round struck sparks from the RAV4's roof, the vehicle was turning out of sight onto a side street, disappearing before he could fire another shot.

Furious at himself, he told the other members of his team, "I lost them, damn it! Watch for others wherever you are. I'm blind up here."

That was not strictly true, of course. He had an unobstructed view of Suds and Bubbles, what was left of it, and a direct line toward the second floor, albeit with thick curtains pulled across the windows, hiding whoever was up there and whatever they were doing now.

A heartbeat later, even with the drapes drawn tight, he got the gist from muzzle flashes dancing on the curtains, gunshots echoing across the street, then bullets shattering the windows from inside. Hardy was torn between descending, heading over in a rush to join the fight, or following his orders and remaining where he was, to watch the street.

"Come on, for God's sake!" he beseeched the night. "Somebody answer me!"

Stan Dartnell followed the Mahoney brothers upstairs to their second-story target, pausing when Reg Hardy's voice came through the Bluetooth earpieces announcing trouble on the street in front. One of the brothers made a curt acknowledgement before they rushed ahead, kicked through an access door, and disappeared inside the *llello* cutting plant.

Dartnell was torn between following orders, staying with the brothers, or delaying on the staircase long enough to see if enemies were coming up behind them from the street. He lingered, heard wild bursts of automatic fire emerging from the laundromat downstairs, and thought of Nat Karpin alone, facing whatever had befallen her in Suds and Bubbles.

"Bugger this!" he told the empty stairwell, torn between his duty and the call of friendship.

Before he could settle anything, three things happened at once.

First, gunfire echoed from the upstairs cutting lab, accompanied by women's screams and men cursing in Spanish Dartnell couldn't understand.

Second, besides the shooting from downstairs, a sharp explosion rocked the building, almost certainly the detonation of a hand grenade.

And third, a group of men carrying automatic carbines and shotguns barged through the door Dartnell had entered fleeting moments earlier, prepared to storm the stairs.

Whatever choice he might have made was taken from him now. The only thing that Stan could do was hold his ground, prevent the new arrivals from surprising Grant and Blake Mahoney in the cutting lab.

Without another second's hesitation, Dartnell cut loose with his AK-9, triggering three-round bursts that dropped the first *sicario* in line and sent his comrades lurching back downstairs in search of any cover they could find. There wasn't much before they hit the outer sidewalk, but their stubby carbines opened fire and one assassin's twelve-gage blue out ceiling panels above Dartnell's head, cascading dust and mutilated vinyl plastic.

Stan ripped another burst out of his AK-9 and saw another narcotrafficker go down, clutching a bloody arm.

Before the three remaining gunmen could react to that, he turned and bolted up the stairs, then through a door that opened on the cutting plant.

The back-and-forth of firing had subsided there, a haze of gun smoke hanging in the air despite a throbbing air-conditioner at work. "Smokeless" gunpowder had been widely used around the world since its first introduction in the 1920s, but the name was a misnomer. Gunpowder, in fact, had not been "powder" since the fourteenth century, and its "smokeless" form—designed to keep from blinding soldiers or betraying their positions with great clouds of whitish smoke—can only be produced by pelletizing or extruding granular material employed as a propellant which, unlike traditional black powder, deemed a "low" explosive, does not detonate but rather *deflagrates*, burning quickly but at subsonic speed.

That said, it was impossible to fire a gun repeatedly, much less numerous guns withing a claustrophobic space, without some smoke fouling the air. Combatants smell it at the scene of any battle, "sport" shooters are familiar with the wisps of smoke that issue from their weapons' muzzles after firing.

Chalk that up in the same column that calls sound suppressors "silencers," even when shots are audible to some extent from yards away. As for the movie mills of Hollywood where "silencers" mute the reports of open-frame revolvers, shrug that off as total fantasy.

Dartnell glanced back the way he'd come and found the stairwell vacant. Those who'd tried to kill him had bailed out and dragged their dead or wounded after them into the night. In front of him, four guards lay dead, scattered around the layouts blood-slick vinyl floor. Two of the cutters lay beside them, while four others stood against a wall dressed only in their underwear, hands raised above their heads.

Neither Mahoney brother was a fluent Spanish-speaker, but they knew enough from hanging out in Southern California to communicate the basics. "*¡Sal ahora mientras puedas!*" Grant commanded.

Get out now while you still can!

The four survivors bolted past Dartnell and down the stairs, none pausing to retrieve their street clothes. How they might explain near-nudity if intercepted by police was up to them and not Stan's problem.

"Nat?" asked Blake Mahoney.

"We should check on her," Dartnell replied. "She blew the laundromat."

"We noticed," Grant advised.

"I haven't seen her sense and she's not answering Hardy."

"All right," the elder brother said. "Let's torch this shit and hit the road before somebody calls the cops or cartel reinforcements."

Road flares did the trick, after Blake and Dartnell splashed jugs of chemicals over the mounds of crystal flake laid out on cafeteria-style tables in the middle of the room. In seconds flat the hungry flames were spreading, raising clouds of smoke that would induce a contact high if they remained to watch the place burn down.

Natalie met them on the sidewalk, looking flushed but otherwise unharmed.

"Two down for me," she said. "I couldn't tell you who they were. No I.D.s in their pockets when their buddies bailed."

"Not friends of Pablo, though," Grant said, "considering the way they came in heavy."

"No," Dartnell agreed. "Looks like we've stepped into the middle of a war."

Blake smiled as they retreated to their rented vehicles and answered, "I can live with that."

8

Granizal, Medellín

Sometimes Felipe Ortiz hated telephones. They seemed to lie in wait for him and interrupt his pleasant times too often—partying, engaged in sex, enjoying sports events—and never seemed to bring good news on those occasions, only headaches and an extra load of work involving danger to himself.

Tonight, however, was the very worst.

This time it was El Tigre's turn to make the call, deliver grim tidings of failure in the mission he had been assigned, hoping that his volatile *padrino*--Joaquín Cardenas Sanchez, better known as *El Aniquilador*, "The Annihilator"—would not blame him for the upset in their plans and sentence him to death by slow torture, along with every other member of his dwindling family.

Ortiz drank two stiff shots of rum and barely felt them before dialing the number of his *jefe* in Guadalajara, capital of Jalisco on Mexico's Pacific coast. He listened to it ring six times, twenty-one hundred miles away from where he sat, before a man's gruff voice he did not recognize answered, *"¿Qué deseas?"*

What did El Tigre want, indeed?

He would have loved to let someone else bear the news

and take whatever punishment Joaquín Cardenas Sanchez thought it merited, but that was not an option. He, Felipe Ortiz, had been in charge—still was, in fact—and if the axe fell, it would be upon his neck.

"An urgent call from Medellín for *Don* Cardenas."

"*Un momento.*"

The distant phone was placed on hold, the best part of another minute slipping past before his master's voice came on the line. "Felipe. *¿Qué pasa?*"

In simple sentences, El Tigre laid out what had happened, making no excuses for himself. Four of the soldiers he had started out with had been killed by *gringo* interlopers, so far unidentified. A fifth *sicario* was badly wounded, might lose use of his left arm unless a trauma surgeon was obtained. Their target was destroyed but Ortiz still admitted that the clash must be regarded as a loss for the Guadalajara Cartel. In order to proceed, El Tigre needed reinforcements from Jalisco.

When he'd finished laying out the facts, Cardenas let another ninety seconds pass before he spoke again. Sitting far from home, in his Hotel Conquistadores suite on Calle 543 in Granizal, a far-northeastern neighborhood of Medellín, Ortiz kept silent, swallowing the urge to ask if he could make it right or if he might as well just put a pistol in his mouth right now.

At last, Cardenas spoke again. His voice seemed calm—not always a good sign, as Ortiz knew from personal experience—but questioning.

"*Estos gringos,*" he said. "You have no clue who they might be?"

"Not yet, *jefe.*" Ortiz had saved the worst for last. "From what was seen and heard, I estimate there must be four or five of them at least. Some of my soldiers say three men. The only one I saw was *una mujer.*"

At the far end of the line, Cardenas laughed at that, a harsh and disconcerting sound. "You got your ass kicked by a woman, eh? That must be so embarrassing, Felipe."

"To be fair, *jefe,* she carried some kind of machine gun and set off a hand grenade."

"A feisty *coño.* I admire that. It's a shame that I hired you instead of her, eh?"

Ortiz offered no reply to that, knowing that it would only stoke his master's rage.

Cardenas sounded almost bored when he inquired, "And what of this supposed Pablo Escobar reborn? Have you discovered where to find him yet?"

"Soon, *jefe,* I believe. That is, if you allow me to continue."

No hesitation this time, as Cardenas asked him, "And why should I?"

"Because I have never failed you in the past," Ortiz replied. "I will not say that I deserve the chance to put this right—"

"Nor would I, Felipe."

"But if you permit it, I will make you proud of me again. And afterward, if you still wish to punish me, I am at your disposal."

An eternal moment later, *Don* Cardenas said, "*Bien.* You have another chance, Felipe, but it will be your last. And I expect reports of progress very soon. *Muy pronto, entiendes?*"

"*Sí, jefe.* About those reinforcements…"

The sigh that came to him across the line reminded Ortiz of a dragon growling in its sleep.

"I'll send another six men off tonight. If you lose them, or any of the rest, expect to offer up one life for each of theirs."

"It's only fair, *patron. Mil gracias* for being merciful."

"Don't thank me yet, Felipe. First, let's see if you survive."

Ortiz was fumbling in his mind for a reply when *Don* Cardenas cut the link and left a dial tone buzzing in his ear.

Click Clack Hotel

The SFX team had convened in Grant Mahoney's suite, dining on room service and hashing over details of their first move against the resurgent Medellín Cartel. The only good news, so far, was that none of them had suffered any injuries besides some minor bruising that Nat Karpin shrugged off as irrelevant.

Leaping around a laundromat and dodging automatic fire before she blew the joint away could do that to a lady.

"Job one," Grant told them, "is identifying the *sicarios* who dropped in on our party uninvited."

"They didn't work for Escobar or whatever he calls himself when he's at home," Reg Hardy said. "They came in hard, before any of his lot could have called for backup."

"Too right," Stan Dartnell chimed in. "Those wankers came in gunning for the home team, not supporting it."

"Agreed," Grant said. "So, who were they?"

"Take your pick," said brother Blake Mahoney. "He's been taking out rival Colombians, trespassing into Mexico, and squeezing out Bolivians. That's quite a list of pissed-off *narcotrafficantes*."

"And we need to trim it down," Grant said, "before we can address it satisfactorily."

"I'd have asked them for a business card," Natalie quipped, "but I was otherwise engaged."

That got a laugh from Dartnell and a smile from Hardy, but the moment quickly passed.

"We need to whittle down that list," Grant said. "Can't have the other hostiles dropping in whenever they feel like it, getting in our way."

"Is there a bonus if we take on two cartels at once?" asked Hardy, sounding serious.

"I'll have a word with Preston Chandler, find out what he knows about it," Grant advised, "but my guess is that he'll be in the dark as much as we are."

"Or he'll lie and claim he is," Blake said.

"You still don't trust him." Natalie addressed herself to Blake.

"It's not just him," the SFX vice president replied. "The DEA puts up a decent fight most of the time, but they're surrounded by corruption and temptation constantly. They're only human, after all, from the director's office right on down the line."

"So, we can't even be sure that we're working for the good guys," Hardy said.

"That needs attention," Grant admitted, "but we know damned well that the cartels are bad across the board. We need to focus on the mission we agreed to: try to find out who this so-called Pablo is, in fact, and take him down if feasible. Beyond that, anyone who tries to stop us is an enemy."

"And we can take 'em out," Blake said.

"Bearing in mind that this is still Colombia," his brother interjected. "If we're caught, their laws apply, and we can't plead collaboration with the DEA. Worst case scenario, we could wind up like Kiki Camarena. If we go to jail down here, it won't be party time at *La Catedral*. Anyone who wants to bail out, this would be the time."

The moment of decision came and went. No member of the team expressed desire to catch the next flight out of Medellín for home, wherever that might be. Grant scanned their solemn faces, nodded finally, and said, "Okay. We're still all in."

"Next stop?" Natalie asked him.

"Chandler's man gave up an address where he thinks our primary target may hang his hat from time to time. Or, anyway, hook up with ladies when he's got the time to spare."

"A love nest?" Hardy said. "I doubt he'll have much

use for it right now."

"Still couldn't hurt to have a look inside," Grant said. "We might find something that will put us closer to him. At the very least, trespassing on his private space could give our guy a case of nerves."

"And push him into a mistake," Dartnell remarked.

"One nice *fatal* mistake," Blake said.

"One's all we need," Grant said.

"And if there's time," said Natalie, "maybe another heart-to-heart with Claudio Román."

"Or double-check his bona fides with Preston at the very least," Hardy put in.

"So, lots to do, then," Grant agreed. "First thing tomorrow good for everyone?"

"Before the cock crows suits me fine," Dartnell advised.

"Hey, keep it clean Down Under," Natalie cautioned.

"I do my best," the Aussie quipped.

"How does four hours sleep sound, then we hit the bricks around sunrise?" Grant asked.

The other SFX members nodded agreement in their turn. It made a short night's rest, but each of them had grown accustomed to long and erratic hours with their military agencies and nothing much had changed since they signed on with Strike Force X. People or agencies that needed help from specialists commonly needed it without delay.

In private paramilitary contracting, the rule had always been, you snooze, you lose.

Often it came down to you snooze, you die in some unpleasant way.

Not that Grant knew of any pleasant, warm and fuzzy way to shuffle off the mortal coil, though some were worse than others he could mention.

So far, during their trip to Medellín, at least five men had died—or maybe six, if the last guy Dartnell had wounded lost his bid to stay alive after the Suds and Bubbles dustup.

Grant Mahoney wished he had a fix on who they were, how many more were circulating through the city and environs at that moment, waiting to jump in and join the game when they were least expected.

Life inside a shooting gallery was hazardous, but it was never dull.

"Till five o'clock then," he reminded his companions as they rose to file out of his suite, returning to their own. "Game faces on, ready for anything."

Los Colores, Medellín

Jorge Torrenegra kept his phone calls to a bedrock minimum, keenly aware of how his enemies, both in and out of government, took pride in tapping, hacking, using whatever advanced technology was deemed the very latest thing, to put his long-range plans at risk.

Torrenegra—or Pablo Escobar, as he preferred to be identified these days—had a closet at home which held nothing but cell phones, still in boxes, all of them identical prepaid "burners," each used for one call only with a scrambling device attached, then crushed and burned, thereby rendered untraceable. If law enforcement crashed his current home one day and found a mass of melted wire and plastic in the bowels of his basement incinerator, it would be no help to them.

Besides, if that should come to pass, that man who would be Medellín's new King of Cocaine would almost certainly be dead.

Tonight's call was occasioned by a grim emergency. He placed it from his library at home, eyeing the shelves of books he'd never read and likely never would, preferring them as status symbols to impress rare visitors than as classical tools for broadening his mind.

Brigadier General Raül Sandino answered on the second ring at home. He sounded tipsy, or perhaps he'd just been on the verge of dozing off. In either case, in made no difference.

"*¿Hola?*" he said.

"No names," said Torrenegra before any more could pass between them. "Is this line secure?"

The brigadier came wide awake, or maybe sobered up. "Of course," he said. Added, "This is…unusual."

"It is unique and won't happen again," the narcotrafficker advised. "Are you aware of what's been happening tonight?"

"Perhaps a bit more detail, if you please."

"The laundromat in Las Penitas," Torrenegra answered.

"No. I've been told nothing yet."

"The fire brigade has come and gone. There were fatalities. I'm positive of seven, but *policía* will have to rake the ashes after sunrise."

"If I understand you, this was not an accident? With all the chemicals…"

"No accident. It was a hostile action, but with a surplus of enemies."

Sandino took a moment, trying to make sense of that, then said, "I do not follow you."

"From what I hear, one group attacked but then was interrupted, driven off by someone more adept. It seems that one group came upon the other by surprise. In any case, before they left one faction or the other set the place afire. Nothing was saved."

"Perhaps that's for the best," the brigadier replied. "Nothing remains to trace by means of title searches, then."

"I'm not that foolish," Torrenegra said. "And that is not the reason why I'm speaking to you now."

"Oh, no? *¿Cuál es la razón, entonces?*"

"The reason, General, is that I pay you, and quite handsomely you must admit, in order for you to protect me from such incidents."

"And I have always done so in the past," Sandino said.

"The past is simply that: the past. I needed you *tonight*, or better still, before my enemies invaded Antioquia without a hint of warning from your agency."

"*Señor,* you know Passport Control and Immigration are not handled by the National Police directly."

"And we both know, General, that you and your subordinates maintain surveillance on a range of felons, terrorists, and *narcotrafficantes*, even if it's only to extract your bribes along the way."

"If you are trying to suggest—"

"I suggest nothing," Torrenegra interrupted him. "I'm stating it directly. We have an arrangement, signed and sealed. If you are now unable to continue as before, I'll have to find somebody else to take your place. And naturally, I'll expect a refund of the payments you've received to cover this year, starting from tonight. Cash is acceptable."

"It is unwise of you to threaten me," Sandino warned.

"I never threaten anyone," the cartel leader said. "I *do* make promises and keep my word without exception to the friends who serve me well. But if they fail me…"

"What? You'll kill me, then? Is that your message?"

"Such a crude insult from one who should know better. Do you not recall the fate of Venezuela's *Cartel de los Soles*, General?"

Sandino seemed to choke on that. The *Cartel de los Soles*—Cartel of the Suns, in English—earned its name because its leaders were commanding officers in the Armed Forces of Venezuela, nicknamed for the golden sunburst emblems pinned onto their epaulets. For years on end they ran their homeland's cocaine trade, protecting shipments, loading trucks and airplanes, killing off the smaller rivals of their partners in the business. Finally, in 2015, DEA agents and prying journalists exposed the syndicate, resulting in disgrace and indictment of various high-ranking officers, including Néstor Reverol, head of the Bolivarian National Guard, and Hugo Carvajal, former head of Venezuelan Military Intelligence.

After a long moment of silence, Brigadier Sandino answered back, "You have no evidence supporting such a charge."

"Are you quite sure of that?" asked Torrenegra. "Absolutely, positively certain in your mind and heart? Would you prefer to call my bluff, as *gringos* say?"

A long moment of silence followed, then Sandino asked, in a defeated tone, "What is it you require?"

"The names of those attempting to destroy us both, their points of origin, and where they may be found in Medellín. I know that you shall find a way to solve this problem for us, Brigadier. *Buenas noches y duerme bien.*"

In fact, he doubted that Sandino would enjoy a good night or sleep well.

And frankly, Torrenegra didn't give a damn.

20 de Julio District, Medellín

Camilo Román had decided it was time for him to get away from Medellín for good, perhaps to leave Colombia entirely if he could finagle that with the resources at his fingertips.

His handler at the DEA, the ever-solemn Preston Chandler, had discouraged that intention when they spoke by telephone, some ninety minutes earlier. In fact, he had forbidden it explicitly, advising Román that "things might go badly" for him if he tried to cut and run just now, with an important project in the works and secret contractors from the United States in Antioquia, stirring up a real *tormenta de mierda*.

Storm of shit that was, in English, but Román preferred

the lilting language of his birth.

In either tongue, of course, the net result stank to high heaven and beyond.

So he was getting out, despite Chandler's transparent threats, coupled with offers of a further feeble stipend for his efforts if he stayed and saw the mission through. Feigning reluctance, Román had agreed, though he had no intention of complying under pressure when his life was certainly at stake.

Now was the time to leave, and if he waited any longer, it would likely be too late.

The neighborhood in which his small apartment was located bore the name of Colombia's Independence Day, celebrated nationwide on July 20th of each successive year. The actual event dated from 1810, when liberator Simón Bolívar had triumphed in his struggle free both Colombia and Venezuela from rule by the Viceroyalty of New Granada after seven decades of oppressive servitude. The end result, called Gran Colombia had encompassed much of northern South America in 1831, including the territories of present-day Colombia, Ecuador, Panama and Venezuela, plus portions of northern Peru, western Guyana and northwestern Brazil. That was the reason why the Isthmus of Panama still featured prominently on Colombia's national seal, although the nations had been separate now for the better part of 190 years.

Old memories died hard, but they were only ancient history.

Román was more concerned about the future now, specifically his own.

He had no relatives in Medellín, no one for Preston Chandler or the drug cartels to use against him as intimidation, holding him in bondage as their puppet. He had cash enough to buy fake travel papers, and his old used car would get him to the nearest border and beyond. From there…well, he would run until he found a place to rest, then wait and see if anyone came looking for him.

And if so, he would to everything within his power to defend himself.

Failing at that, then he would die, as all men ultimately must.

Román finished packing the few clothes he would carry with him, latched his battered plastic suitcase, slipped on a well-worn bomber jacket he had picked up on the cheap from a used-clothing kiosk in El Hueco, in El Centro, offering the lowest prices readily available in Medellín. He also donned a hat that made him look vaguely like Indiana Jones—a poor man's version, not to be confused with any leading man from Hollywood—and looked around his small apartment one last time, to see if he'd forgotten anything.

Nothing he wished to carry with him into limbo, anyway.

Román crossed to the door and opened it, recoiling as he found a husky stranger in a hooded sweatshirt standing there, blocking his path.

"*¿Quién eres tú?*" he asked. "Who are you looking for?"

"*Para ti, creo,*" the stranger said. "Are you not Claudio Román?"

"You are mistaken," Román lied. "Someone has given you the wrong address, I think." His right hand drifted down and backward toward the knife sheathed on his belt. "There must be some mistake."

"Your lies don't work on me, *cobarde.*"

And as if from nowhere, Román's nameless caller raised a pistol, muzzle-heavy with an oblong sound suppressor. When it fired at point-blank range, the bullet punched through Román's left eye socket, toppling his corpse onto the short-nap, threadbare carpet of his former living room, where he would never live again.

9

Manrique, Medellín

The Guerreros del Camino Trucking Company—"Road Warriors" in translation, likely someone's notion of a joke—was owned by Pablo Escobar reborn, if SFX could trust the word of Camilo Román, but the team checked it out anyway, taking nothing for granted since last night's fiasco at Suds and Bubbles.

"These guys like their fun with names," said Blake Mahoney, as his brother piloted their rented auto on an early morning drive-by past the fenced in lot and warehouse.

Both brothers had learned enough Spanish in high school to get by in basic conversation, but they'd never be mistaken for natives south of the border, either by appearance or their fluency. Deployment to "The Sand" and other hot spots on the far side of the world had prompted hit-and-miss linguistic studies with a greater chance of hoping them survive in the Levant and farther east.

"Simple amusements for a bunch of simple minds," Grant said. "It wouldn't pay to underestimate them, though."

"Or whoever's trying to take their boss man down."

"I'd say that fence is what, ten feet before you hit the razor wire?"

"Sounds right," Grant said. "But no signs claiming its

electrified, at least."

"CCTV posted at intervals of thirty yards. Let's hope whoever's in there will be taking a siesta now," Blake countered.

As if in answer to that spoken thought, they saw a rust-speckled garage door rising, rolling back into the cavernous garage, as swarthy men began emerging from the office. All were armed and making no attempt to hide the fact, some carrying assault weapons, all fidgeting with pistols tucked under their belts to make the guns more comfortable.

Grant slowed down and turned a corner, parking in the shadow of a tired-looking Brazil nut tree. With Blake, he watched the early risers—eight in all, with one guy giving orders and gesticulating—break off into teams. Appointed drivers climbed into the cabs of semi-tractor rigs and cranked the diesel engines over, while their partners ducked into the warehouse, out of sight. It took some awkward jockeying, but one by one, the tractor units backed into the warehouse, under pale fluorescent ceiling lights, and rolled back out with trailers hitched onto their fifth wheels, spewing noxious fumes into the morning air from overhead exhaust pipes.

Grant got on the walkie-talkie, gave his scattered teammates the heads-up. "Looks like we've got a convoy rolling out. Could be a bonus."

"Works for me," Reg Hardy answered.

"I'm on top of it," Natalie Karpin chimed in.

"Who's seen the movie *Road Games*?" Stan Dartnell queried. "Nobody? Stacy Keach and Jamie Lee Curtis tracking a maniac from Adelaide to Perth?"

"Sounds like a classic," Nat replied.

Dartnell snorted and said, "You're all a bunch of Philistines."

"Look sharp and settle down," Grant cautioned all of them. "We don't know where they're headed, so we'll need to take advantage of terrain and minimize the danger to civilians."

"What if they split up?" asked Hardy. "Are we even sure they're carrying?"

"Trusting our informant to a point," Grant told the team. "They aren't packing that hardware to protect a load of microwaves and dishwashers."

"Fair point, mate," Dartnell granted.

"If they run in tandem, we close in and pick them off," Grant said. "If some of them break off, use your best judgment. Stay in touch whichever way it breaks."

Acknowledgements came in from all concerned, before their radios switched off. They'd settled on a frequency Grant deemed unlikely for a trucking outfit's CB radios to monitor but that came down to guesswork in the end. Radio silence was the way to go for safety's sake, with cryptic contact held to a bare minimum.

A gunman with an AK-47 slung over his shoulder started rolling back the tall gate in the fence that ringed the Guerreros del Camino property. The eighteen-wheelers started moving out in tandem, following a Peterbilt with two men in the cab, each rig behind the leader with another two *sicarios* on board. When the last semi was clear, the gate rolled shut again, and those employees left behind trooped back inside the office.

"Party time," said Blake Mahoney, as his brother let the last rig pass, then joined the convoy from two blocks behind.

Around them, out of sight and following or running parallel, the other SFX team members kept pace with the parade, three cars in all. Grant didn't have to warn them about holding back in densely populated neighborhoods where any strike could turn into an all-out massacre.

Trailing the final truck in line, Kenworth, Grant asked Blake, "How's the romantic getaway been treating you?"

Blake snorted. Said, "I've never been a fan of make-believe."

"Cold-shoulder time?"

"We may be in the tropics, bro, but I'm not feeling any heat."

"Just wait," Grant said. "With any luck, we've got some coming up."

From Manrique the procession traveled east, then northward toward Veredas Granizal, although that rural suburb was not meant to be the convoy's destination. If all went to plan, the semis would be stopping sooner, without entering the settlement that had become ground zero between warring bandit clans, recording weekly homicides that rivaled any other part of Medellín.

Victor Giraldo, placed in charge of the delivery hoped the *bandidos* would be wise enough to give his soldiers a side berth. He did not fear police as much as numskulls who were bold and dumb enough to rob a major shipment with the dual hopes of getting rich and building up a reputation for ferocity.

In either case, if someone tried it, Giraldo was determined eradicate them without giving it a second thought.

He worried over last night's trouble at the laundromat and cutting plant in Las Penitas. While Giraldo was not privy to his *jefe*'s thoughts and schemes, he clearly recognized a major challenge to the growing strength and reputation of the man he knew as Pablo Escobar revived by means beyond his understanding.

Not that perfect understanding was required. Giraldo, like the great majority of his *amigos* in the drug trade, had been raised on superstition, reverence for *orishas* who ostensibly controlled all things, despite the chaos found in daily life throughout Colombia. He did not rule out resurrection of the dead, but scarcely cared if it was fact or fiction.

When a leader came along who could command the loyalty of hardened men, put money in their pockets and advance then in a vicious cutthroat trade, wise soldiers followed him and honored him with fealty—at least until another, stronger overlord rose up to take his place.

Survival was the art of looking out for Number One.

The walkie-talkie on Giraldo's hip crackled. He recognized the caller's voice as that of Santiago Betancourt, the last driver in line, his urgency apparent even through the scratchy radio's receiver.

"We have company," Betancourt said.

"*¿Que tipo de compañia?*" Giraldo asked.

"Two cars, at least," Betancourt answered. "Maybe more. I can't be positive."

"*¡Chinga tu madre!*" Victor blurted out the curse. "How many people altogether?"

"Two men in the first car," the reply came back. "I can't be sure about the other."

Giraldo's driver, Carlos Obregon, shot him a nervous glance. Asked him, "What should we do, Victor?"

"More men are waiting for us at the airstrip," said Giraldo, reaching for the CB radio mounted above the tractor's useless rearview mirror. "I'll alert them. If these *hijos de puta* make a move before we get there, then we fight."

With his left hand, Victor snared the CB microphone and pulled it toward his lips, thumbed down the button labeled "SEND" and spoke into it. "Powder Train to Eagle's Nest. *¡Responde de inmediato!*"

In his lap, Giraldo's right hand rested on an Uzi submachine gun, full-sized, with its stock folder, loaded with a forty-round box magazine. His backup weapon, nestled in a shoulder holster hidden by hit lightweight jacket, was a Browning Hi-Power pistol chambered for the same 9×19mm Parabellum rounds as the compact Israeli SMG. Beside him, Carlos had an MP5K machine pistol resting on the cab's bench seat, similar in length to Victor's Uzi but with two forty-round magazines taped end-to-end for quick reloading.

Each team in the trucks behind them carried similar

hardware—rifles and submachine guns, shotguns, all with pistols in reserve. Each man had proved himself a killer in the past and might again this morning, sometime in the next few minutes.

"Eagle's Nest to Powder Train. I read you. Over?"

"We have trackers," Victor warned the narcotrafficker in charge of loading and dispatching planes. He had a Cessna CitationJet/M2 on standby, waiting to take on the *llello* en route from Manrique and ferry it to the Bahamas, once the kilo packages had been removed from cheap TV sets where they lay concealed.

Now all that was in jeopardy.

"What do you need from us?" the airstrip manager inquired.

"Be ready to receive them if they get that far," Giraldo answered. "Have men on standby if they stop us earlier."

"You'll signal us in that event?"

"*Voy a.* How many can you spare?"

"Seven *sicarios,* plus twelve men from the loading crew."

"*Bueno.* Prepare them now."

"*Tal como dices.* Out!"

The airfield still lay seven or eight miles ahead. Checking his wing mirror, Giraldo finally spotted the first pursuit car, some late-model sedan he could not recognize offhand. It had begun to tailgate the last truck in line, and now it swerved from sight, as if trying to pass.

"It's happening," he cautioned Obregon.

"What if they are *la policía,* Victor?"

"*¡A la mierda!* Pigs die, just like anybody else."

Natalie Karpin, riding solo in the second chase car, watched as the Mahoney brothers changed lanes, rocketing along to pass the final truck in line. She wasn't sure precisely what they had in mind but knew that contact was about to happen with all parties traveling at sixty miles per hour, rapidly accelerating.

Karpin didn't need to check the AK-9 carbine riding beside her, knowing it was cocked and locked, only depression of its safety catch required to let her join the coming fight. Exactly what form that would take she couldn't say but hurtling along a rural two-lane highway in pursuit of half a dozen eighteen-wheelers packed with drugs and God knew what else did not boost her confidence.

She wasn't *worried,* mind you, but wise soldiers—the survivors—always realized they weren't invincible.

As the Mahoney brothers overtook the convoy's final rig, that truck's driver angled a pistol toward them through his open window, fired left-handed, but his shots missed by a yard or more. Before the wheelman could correct his aim, the brothers were running beside the next-to-last big rig, with Blake Mahoney spraying short bursts from his AK-9.

Instead of aiming for the cab, Blake targeted the trailer's rear tires on the driver's side, his 9×39mm rounds fired from a yard or less away punching through rubber, causing an explosive decompression of the ruptured tires. At once, as Grant Mahoney picked up speed and powered clear, the crippled trailer fishtailed, yawing wildly back and forth, before it jackknifed and collapsed onto its left-hand side, trailing a plume of sparks and fragments of torn asphalt.

Natalie accelerated automatically, swung wide across the southbound lane and up onto its shoulder, plowing ruts in grass and dirt there. When she'd cleared the toppled wreckage, she veered back onto the highway proper, chasing SFX's CEO and Veep along what still remained of the drug convoy.

In her rearview mirror, for a fleeting moment, Natalie beheld the final truck as it collided with the toppled trailer, air brakes screaming their mechanical alarm, which made the former mess a two-truck pileup that would call for heavy cranes to clear the road again.

The sabra warrior couldn't stop herself from grinning, but she swallowed an impulse to cheer aloud. Four eighteen-wheelers were still rolling, each manned by at least two narcotraffickers apiece, and no one on the SFX team knew where they were headed yet. If even one got through, their mission would have failed and they would be no closer to the man who posed before the underworld as Pablo Escobar reborn, little the worse for wear.

A clean sweep was required, and preferably with a captive they could grill for answers someplace well removed from what had now become a highway battleground.

And failing that, she thought, the smugglers had to be wiped out, their poison earmarked for the States destroyed before it ruined any further lives.

Grim-faced after her brief elation, Karpin powered down the window on her rental's right-hand side, picked up her AK-9 carbine, and leaned across to prop its muzzle on the padded windowsill. Her turn was coming, and she meant to make it count.

Reg Hardy had to navigate around four jackknifed eighteen-wheelers as he sped to join the other members of the SFX squad.

Passing the second pair of tangled rigs along the way, he saw a bloodied figure lurching out to meet him, shotgun raised to fire, but Hardy hit him with a three-round burst from his Kalashnikov and put him down.

It wasn't sniping from a distance, but whatever worked was satisfactory, as long as Hardy wasn't killed or wounded in the process.

Posting cars ahead of the cocaine convoy would have resolved that difficulty, but without a clue to the transporters' destination, that had been impossible. Reg still had no idea where they'd been headed, but smart money said it had to be a private airstrip tucked away somewhere nearby, knowing only an idiot would try to move a truck convoy from Medellín to some transshipment point in an adjoining country with what must be tons of *llello* stashed on board.

Of course, they hadn't seen the coke yet, but that made no difference to Reg. Even without a look inside, he was convinced the trucks *were* hauling drugs. Why else would they need two guards each with automatic weapons? Even the most hare-brained, wired-up bandits in Colombia weren't going to attack a convoy hauling televisions, freezers or whatever when they'd have nowhere to hide them and no means of fencing them besides.

Ahead of him, Reg saw the last—or *first*—two semis in the caravan had stopped dead in the middle of the two-lane blacktop, although neither one of them had crashed. The leading rig had three or four of its ten tires shredded by gunfire but had wallowed to a halt, rims gouging furrows in the asphalt, while its trailer swung around to block both lanes but hadn't flipped.

The rig behind that one was stopped and idling, with its driver possibly considering some way of breaking free, but he was going nowhere with the road blocked fore and aft. Hardy arrived behind that semi, bailed out of his rented ride, and ended any prospect of escape with two quick AK bursts that left the trailer's punctured rear tires hissing like a nest of angry snakes.

Carbine ready, Reg stepped from his car. He had already seen Natalie Karpin and the two Mahoney brothers up ahead, exchanging fire with someone in the point rig. Now, another revving engine at his back made Hardy turn as Stan Dartnell arrived and braked his rental to a halt.

"What's happening?" their last arrival queried, as he left his vehicle to join Reg in the second eighteen-wheeler's shadow.

"You can see as much as I do," Hardy answered. "Couldn't see a point to interrupting them with jibber-jabber on the radio."

"Right, then," the Aussie said. "I'm moving in. You want to tag along?"

Before they could advance, though, two men bailed out of the tractor-trailer nearest to them, firing from the hip as they touched down.

Grant and Blake Mahoney sprayed the last rounds from their AK carbine magazines into the point rig's bullet-punctured cab, then switched to fresh mags while Natalie Karpin covered them. Return fire from inside the cab had stopped, at least for now, but no one on the SFX team felt like taking anything for granted.

Shooting from the second truck in line distracted them, the *pop* of carbines from their late-arriving teammates, answered by the waspish rattle of a submachine gun and the *boom* of what was probably a twelve-gauge. Glancing off in that direction, without drawing full attention from the Peterbilt in front of him, Grant saw Dartnell and Hardy squaring off against a couple of *sicarios* who'd manned the second rig in line.

That didn't last long.

Seasoned killers that they doubtless must have been, the two Colombians were no match for the Brit and Aussie, with their years of training and commando service covering a fair piece of the globe. Within the space of ten or fifteen seconds, tops, both narcotraffickers were down and out, unmoving on the highway's pavement while their blood spread out in ruby-colored pools.

And that left two of their opponents still alive...or maybe not.

Dead silence from the riddled cab, with no return fire in the best part of two minutes, but Grant called out to its occupants, in case that either one of them could hear or felt like answering.

"Inside the Peterbilt! You've got one chance to walk away from this and take a message back to *Don* Pablo. Throw out your weapons. Show yourselves."

No answer, so he tried again in slightly awkward Spanish, waited, and was just about to punctuate his offer with another automatic burst when someone called out from the cab, "You'll only shoot us down, *gringo!*"

"Or I could toss a couple of grenades into your lap, if that's your preference."

"You promise not to shoot?" The question came out as a whine.

"*Lo prometon,*" Grant replied, although he didn't view his word as sacred when he gave it to a homicidal thug. Something he'd picked up from his all-time favorite Western film, *The Wild Bunch*. Ernest Borgnine arguing with William Holden, bellowing, "It ain't your word! It's *who* you give it to!"

Grant had no argument to counter that. He'd seen and done too much to think that anything was "fair," per se.

Fair fights were the ones you walked away from, more or less intact.

"*¡Todo bien!*" the voice called out. "You see our guns, yes?"

Through the nearest open window flew a pair of submachine guns, first any MP5K, then an Uzi.

"And the rest!" Grant ordered.

"*¡Sí, sí!*" A revolver and a semiautomatic pistol followed, bouncing on the pavement as they landed.

"All right," Blake instructed. "Come out slow, one at a time. Try anything and you can kiss your ass goodbye."

The *narcotrafficantes* did as they were told. The driver

led, followed by someone Grant assumed must be the man in charge. The pair stood nervously before five enemies, as Hardy and Dartnell moved up to join the other members of their team.

"Which one of you is *el jefe?*" Grant asked, trying to verify his guess.

The one he had suspected raise a hand. Said, "*Soy.*"

"Okay, then."

Grant lifted his AK-9 and dropped the other where he stood, noting that the confessed leader showed little shock beyond a twitch of his eyebrows. If anything, the sole survivor seemed to be relieved, thinking he might still have a chance.

"Now you're our messenger," Mahoney said. "When you see Pablo, or whatever his father and mother called him, tell him that his time is running out. The best thing he can do is fold his tent and fade away. *¿Entender?*"

"*Sí, señor.* I understand."

"Start walking, then, and don't look back."

Their drafted errand boy resumed his northward journey, now on foot. As he moved out of earshot, Blake Mahoney asked his brother, "What about the load?"

"Can't leave it sitting here," Grant said. "Let's light it up."

10

Manufacturer's brochures describe the Bell 525 Relentless as the "world's most advanced helicopter." And it should be, for the basic retail price of $15 million each.

The aircraft measures fifty-four feet three inches from nose to the tip of its tail, with a main rotor diameter three inches greater than its length. It weighs a fraction under twenty thousand pounds, with seating for two pilots and a maximum of t20 passengers who enter through a pair of large rear sliding doors. Its twin General Electric CT7-2F1 turboshaft engines generate eighteen hundred horsepower apiece, for a cruising speed of 178 miles per hour and a top-end maximum of 190 over a range of 644 miles. Its service ceiling reaches twenty thousand feet.

Jorge Torrenegra loved his helicopter, relished flying over Antioquia in style whenever possible—but not this morning. As he touched down at the airstrip where his convoy of *llello* should be offloading even now, the man who would be Pablo Escobar had murder on his mind.

He only lacked the names and present whereabouts of those he meant to kill.

Well, all but one.

Victor Giraldo waited for him in the airstrip's compact office, coming out to meet the helicopter as it landed, flanked by scowling guards. Clearly, he was a man who knew—or must have guessed by now—that he was running out of time.

Torrenegra disembarked and moved toward the office with his own half-dozen bodyguards. His eyes locked onto Victor's and remained there, while he kept his famous face deadpan, allowing one who'd failed him terribly a moment's shaky hope.

Standing in front of his employee, within arm's length, he simply said, "*Explique.*"

Victor stammered out his explanation, straining past it for some glimpse of an excuse.

"The *gringos* followed us, *jefe*. We did not see them when we left the compound."

"Did not see them?" Torrenegra interrupted. "With so many eyes and the closed-circuit television cameras?"

"They were too well hidden, I suppose, Pablo."

The slap was hard enough to rock Giraldo backward on his heels. One of his guards reached out to keep the worm from falling flat. A livid palmprint marked his cheek.

"Familiarity has robbed you of respect, *carbon.*"

"*¡Perdóname por favor, jefe!*"

"Pardon depends upon your honesty, Victor. Explain what happened to my shipment."

"As I said, the *gringos* followed us, unseen at first, then overtook us on the highway. Gunfire was exchanged."

"I saw the wreckage," Torrenegra said. "How many were there, Victor?"

"Five, in three cars, *jefe*. One of them…" Giraldo hesitated then, as if afraid to speak.

"Tell me! Your difficulty can't grow any worse."

"One of them was a woman," Victor said, his voice

dropping an octave in embarrassment.

"Four *hombres* and a *puta*. Help my memory, Victor. How many of my people did they kill?"

"Eleven, *jefe*. All but me."

"How fortunate for you, eh?" Torrenegra wore a mocking smile. "And why were you spared?"

"To relay a message, *jefe*," Victor cringed before his master.

"So? Tell me."

"*Lo siento much, jefe*. I cannot recall their leader's word exactly."

"Do your best, then," Torrenegra said between clenched teeth.

"I was to say your time is running out. And something else about a tent fading away."

"*¿Una carpa?*"

Giraldo shrugged, a helpless gesture. "*Gringo* nonsense maybe, hoping he could frighten me perhaps."

"Did he succeed, Victor?"

"*¿Jefe?*"

"Were you afraid, with five guns pointed at your face and my *sicarios* all lying dead around you?"

"I suppose so?"

"Are you asking me, *pendejo?*"

"I was worried, *jefe*. I admit it."

"But the murderers released you."

"*Sí*. It was a miracle!"

"Which served their purpose. What about my *llello?*"

"I looked back and saw the trailers burning, *jefe*."

Torrenegra had seen much the same himself, while airborne in the Bell 525, after he got the call from San José la Cima's airfield.

"Do you know what that was worth, between the cargo and the trucks?" Without allowing Victor to reply, he asked, "How will you pay me back?"

"*Jefe,* I don't—"

"No matter," Torrenegra cut him off. He held out his right hand, waiting to clasp the pistol that one of his bodyguards provided.

"*¡Jefe, Perdóname!*" the weasel pled once more.

"This is your pardon, Victor."

As if it were prearranged, Giraldo's flanking guards stepped off a pace in each direction before Torrenegra raised the borrowed gun and fired a shot through Victor's forehead. Blood and gray matter spattered the outer office wall behind him as he fell.

During the hush that followed, Torrenegra said, "Take out the trash," then turned back toward his helicopter, moving with determined strides.

Palace of Justice, Medellín

Brigadier General Raül Sandino flinched a bit to hear the private phone atop his desk clamor for his attention. If he had to guess, Sandino would have said no more than fifteen, maybe twenty of his National Police superiors reached him that way, but certain others also had the number that was meant to be a secret from lesser officials and the public nationwide.

Today, given the news he'd just received from a semi-deserted stretch of highway south of San José la Cima, he'd have bet a month's pay that he knew who must be calling him.

Lifting the telephone receiver, he told whoever it was, "*Espera un momento por favor.*" While they waited a moment, he depressed a button on the phone's dial pad, a small green light illuminated just above it as the built-in scrambler rendered conversation on both sides as gibberish to any eavesdroppers.

"All right," Sandino said when that was done. "The line's secure now."

And the voice that spoke to him was, as expected, that of the supposed Pablo Escobar revived and loosed upon the world again.

"You know about the ambush of my convoy, General?"

"I've only just received the news, with more reports expected momentarily."

"And what have you to say about it?"

"*¿Qué?*" Sandino frowned. "What should I have to say?"

"This is the second strike against me in the past nine hours, General. I now have nineteen people dead, together with a priceless load of merchandise incinerated."

Hardly priceless, thought Sandino. Pricey, yes, but he was sure his caller knew precisely, to the peso or the U.S. dollar, how much it was worth, be that price wholesale or retail on distant street corners.

"*Señor,* my people are investigating and—"

"That's not enough," his caller interrupted. "Two attacks so far, and both involving *gringos,* General, along with the Latinos from last night's fiasco whose identity remains uncertain. You must push your people harder. I require identifies and places where these *hijos de puta* hide between their efforts to destroy our business."

"*¿Nuestro negocio?*" the brigadier replied. "Are we now partners?"

"*Escucha,* General. You've known the rules of our collaboration from the start, when you agreed to offer me protection at a price that guarantees you will retire in luxury. It's too late to pretend confusion now—and much too late for renegotiating price."

"I simply meant—"

"I know *exactamente* what you meant, Raül." Dispensing with Sandino's rank now, in a bid to humble him.

"We settled this last night. If you cannot perform as we agreed…well, then, I must find someone else who can."

"My men are working nonstop on these matters. No one seems to know the *gringos* yet. As for the others—"

"If five *gringos,* all of them professionals, are operating in Colombia today, then someone knows them, knows who sent them. Who would you suspect, offhand?"

"It will not be the FBI," Sandino said. "Most of them are consumed with hunting Arab terrorist and barely pay attention to smugglers at home. As for the CIA, they would more likely try to bargain with you than subvert your trafficking."

"Which naturally leaves the DEA," his caller said.

"Or someone they've employed on their behalf. You know as well as I that private military contractors are all the rage today. I could reel off a list of twelve, perhaps fifteen top operators in the world today, with many times that number struggling for a foothold on the second tier."

"All using former soldiers," Torrenegra said.

"Who may or may not be on file," Sandino answered. "If they served with any kind of special forces in the past, their files are likely classified. Or some of them may be like you."

"Meaning…?"

"In Washington they're known as 'ghosts.' Ex-soldiers listed on the books as killed in action, while they take on new identities, untraceable, and either serve their former governments in that capacity or work as mercenaries anywhere they choose."

"But if their names are known and written down, you could find out which of them recently entered Colombia, *correcto?*"

"It is possible, but not by any means certain."

"Still, if you do not try…"

"I shall resume inquiries when we're finished speaking here."

"Don't let me keep you, then," his caller said and cut the

link. The green light on Sandino's telephone immediately vanished.

Scowling, Sandino slammed a fist down on his desktop blotter, grimaced as it pained his hand, then mouthed a string of curses.

Who was this pretender to insult a man of Raúl Sandino's recognized accomplishments? Who was he to demand that that Sandino risk everything he'd worked for and accumulated all these years in uniform to serve a lowlife *narcotrafficante*?

Simply that, he realized. A cocaine smuggler who could crush Sandino, tear his life apart, simply by sharing what he knew about their mutual relationship for profit. One phone call to the media, one envelope containing transcripts of their conversations, details of the times Sandino had betrayed his oath of office, and there would be nothing left. The brigadier's only escape hatch from a fetid prison cell would then be death by his own hand.

Unless the parasite he served should kill him first.

Better to do as he was told, locate the troublemakers in their midst and give them up to Torrenegra, or perhaps arrange for them to die while "resisting arrest." That almost made the general smile.

Almost.

One thing was certain: death awaited someone in the tangled web surrounding him, and Raül Sandino meant to stall his own demise as long as possible.

José María Córdova International Airport

The six new men from Guadalajara were traveling separately for security's sake, but all still reached Medellín aboard Aeroméxico's flight arriving at noon. The came unarmed, of course, expecting weapons to be furnished at the other end, and all seemed pleased by the equipment their deceased forerunners left behind.

They listened to Felice Ortiz as he explained the details of their mission, none expressing any doubts about the job on which an equal number of the cartel's men—perhaps including some of their *amigos*—had been shot to hell and gone only last night. El Tigre promised them he had the situation well in hand now, watched them nod in bland acceptance of a job like so many they had performed on prior occasions, albeit closer to home.

Ortiz wished that his words were true but dared not voice his own misgivings to these new arrivals. It would shake their confidence and might get back to *Don* Joaquín Cardenas Sanchez in a flash.

When working with an unfamiliar team—or even one well known—El Tigre always took for granted that there was at least one spy among them, likely more than one.

At the hotel, where the new men would occupy suites rented under false names for the recent dead, Ortiz convened them all and spelled out what had happened up to now in Medellín, the stakes involved as they moved forward, and the binding order from their *jefe* that there must be no more "accidents" along the road to ultimate success. El Tigre realized no man could guarantee the future, but he also understood that he who promised satisfactory results must pay a price for failure to deliver.

In this case, that price would be his life.

His first order of business, after showing off their arsenal to his new team members, was feeding them. Room service brought up various hot dishes to El Tigre's suite, where they had gathered: empanadas and *ajiaco* (chicken soup with corn and three kinds of potatoes) for the appetizers; *carne asada* (flank steak marinated in a mixture of beer, citrus and garlic), tamales and *arroz con pollo* for the main course; and flan for dessert.

While they ate, most of them famished since they all agreed that airline foot was *mierda*, Ortiz issued their instructions for the evening ahead.

"I don't know what you have been told," he said. "We face an enemy who styles himself as Pablo Escobar returned from Hell, if you believe such things. *Don* Cardenas puts no stock in such tales, nor do I. We seek a man, no more, no less. To reach him, we must first dismantle the cartel he is attempting to revive, which threatens our *padrino* and the lot of us. If this *imitar* succeeds, he will eclipse the family we serve and none of us will have a future worth enduring."

One of them—scar-faced Aarón Echeverria—voiced a question with his mouth full, while he kept on chewing. "Is it true, *Señor,* that you've already lost six men?"

"*Así es,*" Ortiz granted, showing no embarrassment. "Five dead last night, and one so badly wounded he cannot continue."

Anxious glances shared among the reinforcement indicated they had been forewarned. Echeverria said, "If I may ask, *jefe,* what happened there?"

"It seems that we are not alone in hunting down this fraud who calls himself *Don* Pablo. There are also *gringos* on the prowl in Medellín. We met some of them last night and it turned into a fight between us, being taken by surprise. We won't make that mistake again. As we go forward, be prepared for anything."

"Who sent the *gringos, jefe*?" asked another of his new men, Demian Fuentes, his hair drawn back into a ponytail.

"We don't know that, but *Don* Cardenas is investigating it through government channels. Meanwhile tonight's first target is a nightclub which our enemy is said to own. Whether that's true or not, he sometimes shows himself there. It is called El Gatito."

The Pussycat, that was, translated into *Inglés*. Several of the reinforcements laughed, one of them asking, "So, there should be women there?"

"No doubt," Ortiz replied. "But all of you must keep your eyes and minds on business, eh? That is, if any of you plan on going home alive."

20 de Julio District, Medellín

"This can't be good," said Blake Mahoney, as he turned a corner onto Calle 38 and saw police cars midway down the block, their colored lights revolving, men in uniform standing around outside a small apartment house. An ambulance was parked outside, no sign of its attendants as Mahoney braked and pulled into the curb down range.

"You have the right address?" Natalie Karpin asked.

"It's what he gave us when we met before," Blake said.

Their cover for the side trip was a lovers' tour of Medellín, raising no eyebrows with the Click Clack Hotel's staff. Their mission was to contact Claudio Román and squeeze more information out of him, specifically regarding active opposition to the Pablo Escobar impersonator they were hunting.

Natalie opened the rental's glove compartment and removed a pair of compact field glasses, Nikon's Travelite VI 12x25 binoculars with multicoated optics to provide bright images and glare reduction, central focusing with a clicking diopter control that fine-tuned each eyepiece for strain-free viewing, and aspherical lenses eliminated virtually all distortion. Raising them, she scanned the hectic scene and asked, "What's the apartment number that he gave you?"

"1C," Blake replied.

"It's his place, then," she said, "unless he lied."

"Too risky for a thing like that, in case we'd burn him with his handler."

As Mahoney finished speaking, they could see the ambulance attendants leaving what had been Román's apartment, carrying a stretcher with a plastic body bag on top of it. They stowed their cargo in the meat wagon, slammed its back doors, and drove away as a plainclothes detective exited the ground-floor flat, talking to a young woman in a white coat, carrying a doctor's bag.

"Natural causes, you suppose?" By now, Blake recognized Karpin's sarcastic voice from times he'd spent on its receiving end.

"Get serious," he said.

"Who'd want to take him out just now, one day after you met with him?"

"The short list would be Pablo's people, dirty cops on his payroll, or maybe someone from the crew we met last night at Suds and Bubbles."

"So, too many suspects, then."

"And likely some we haven't thought of yet. If he was diming out one cartel to the DEA and running coke himself, it could be damned near anyone he knew."

One of the officers in uniform had noticed them, drifting in their direction with the indolence that seemed to be standard procedure for Colombian officialdom. Blake spotted him, fired up the rental's engine, and rolled out of there, back toward the Click Clack Hotel in El Poblado.

"Want to call it in?" Natalie asked.

"Better to keep it off the air for now."

Call interception was a fact of life with cell phones in these days when landlines had become passé for many people in developed nations, outside businesses and government facilities that kept multiple lines in play. Programs like FlexiSPY's patented Mobile Spy Software and countless others could snatch conversations from midair, view the activity on tablets such as iPads, Lenovo and Amazon Fire, or track GPS locations without any target catching on.

A mercenary's safest course of action in the field, even with access to a scrambler meant to head off interception and eavesdropping, turned the clock back to the "good old days" of talking face-to-face.

In which case, all you had to think about was stationary bugs, a shotgun microphone, or any one of fifty to a hundred other things.

Simple.

"You know what this means," Natalie reminded Blake.

"That we've been compromised?" he said. "That's what it *could* mean."

"What are the alternatives? Coincidence?"

"It happens sometimes, but I'm no believer in it."

"No," she said. "Neither am I."

"Which leaves whatever enemies Román made for himself, being a narcotrafficker and rat."

"We're back to dirty cops and dealers, then."

"And neither one of those is an endangered species in Colombia, from Bogotá on down the line."

"Which could include the DEA," Karpin observed. "Remember José Irizarry?"

"That scumbag? Who could forget him?" Blake replied.

During his time with DEA, Irizarry had operated between Miami and Cartagena, becoming so immersed in his undercover life that he'd married a Colombian woman and finally sold out to the cartels he was assigned to break, while building up a reputation as an agency "superstar." In the process, he'd conspired with a longtime civilian informant to launder some $7 million through black-market channels over a six-year period. Busted in early 2019, Irizarry and his wife were extradited to face trial in the

United States, but their case was still pending.

Nobody in his right mind thought their case was a one-off fluke. Not with other agents on the books such as Chad Scott, convicted in Louisiana of perjury, obstructing justice and falsifying government records; ex-Marine Fernando Gomez, serving time for leaking DEA files to an outfit called *La Organizacion de Narcotraficantes Unidos*; or "Grant Stentsen," an alias used in Justice Department reports for an agent whose torrid extramarital affair with a convicted cartel felon was tacitly approved by DEA headquarters.

And no one in his right mind thought those four examples were the total list of traitors in the so-called "War on Drugs."

Natalie frowned. Said, "So we have to look at everybody, then."

Blake nodded. "Which includes some we don't even know about, damn it."

Calle 53, Le Candelaria, Medellín

Grant Mahoney was familiar with the red-light zones in Medellín. He'd worked their streets before, not as a "john" but as a hunter, and he knew which streets were lined with strip clubs while *callejeros*—streetwalkers—sought "dates" along the pavement just outside.

Prostitution practiced by consenting adults is legal in Colombia, ostensibly regulated and limited to brothels in designated "tolerance zones," with regular health checks required of all sex workers. Nonetheless, the avenues of La Candelaria, Parque Lleras and Villa Neuva teemed with working girls—and boys—from dusk until the crack of dawn put glaring neon in the shade. Police are rarely seen unless blood spills in public or a corpse is found, the traffic fed by syndicates who prey on victims of the nation's poverty and internal displacement caused by rural violence.

According to UNAIDS—the Joint United Nations Program on HIV/AIDS—Colombia harbors 7,218 known prostitutes, a laughably conservative figure ignoring the nameless, faceless victims of sex trafficking and child-sex racketeering, both illegal on the statute books but seldom interrupted by authorities. And as in any area where sex work flourishes, La Candelaria is also rife with drugs, muggings, and other forms of crime.

While streetwalkers roam at will between Calle 53 and 57, many of their paying customers start out at nude dance clubs found chiefly on Calle 50, Calle 52 and Calle 53. In those joints, strippers bare it all and go for broke on stage, while drinks are overpriced and often watered down—or, in some dives, spiked to relieve unwary tourists of their cash and jewelry.

Eyeing the club they sought tonight, Natalie Karpin read its neon sign aloud. "El Gatito?"

Blake Mahoney translated. "That's 'Pussy Cat'."

"Puh-lease!"

Blake hated to admit it, but the sabra riding with him in their rental car had mastered slang pronunciation from his operating base in Southern California. She could have been a valley girl, except that she had seen more action in the Beqaa Valley and the Golan Heights than on the West Coast of the USA.

"I didn't name the joint," he said. "It's Pablo's dive, or whoever he is."

"According to the late, lamented Claudio Román."

"Is somebody lamenting him?"

Nat didn't answer that. Blake parked his ride in a fenced lot beside the club and came around to hold her door, but she was quicker, already outside the vehicle when he got there. From their selected garb, no casual observer would have known that either one of them was armed. Granted, they couldn't hide their AK-9s conveniently, but Blake carried his Glock in shoulder rigging; Natalie had hers stashed in a slightly oversized handbag.

Grant was already at the door to El Gatito, greeting them like long-lost friends, shaking his brother's hand and grazing Karpin's cheek with a casual kiss. They entered as a trio, after shelling out the mandatory cover charge of twenty thousand pesos each—five U.S. dollars—and receiving stamps depicting a red cat upon their hands.

Inside, the joint was jumping. Or, at least, the naked dancers were, parading on an oval stage resembling a miniature racetrack, each one pausing at multiple stations equipped with steel poles, climbing and writhing as if undergoing some bizarre pelvic exam. Between the poles, the girls paired off, caressing one another, simulating oral sex that lasted for approximately one-third of whatever song was blaring from the club's wall-mounted amplifiers. The tunes, if you could call them that, were mostly Spanish heavy metal, groups like Beholder and Garage snarling their hits such as "*Entrar al Fuego*" and "*Sangre Fuego*"—"Enter the Fire" and "Blood Fire.".

Apparently, their fans were big on fire.

Half-deafened by the throbbing music, Natalie and the Mahoney brothers made their way into the club proper, scanning the patrons and employees. Less than half a minute passed before Grant nudged the others, nodding toward a roped-off second-level mezzanine clearly reserved for VIPs.

Raising his voice, he asked them both, "See what I see?"

They did.

Surrounded by a retinue of babes and bodyguards, there sat a man who could have been the living, breathing twin of Pablo Escobar.

El Tigre passed out wads of pesos to his men, then watched them enter El Gatito singly or in pairs, resembling any other patrons of the club. Women were welcome at the Pussycat but given what it offered in the form of entertainment, 90-odd percent of paying customers were male, ranging in age from eighteen—the alleged cutoff for legal drinking in Colombia—to the onset of doddering senility.

Anyone with twenty thousand pesos to invest could

pass inside and feast his (or her) eyes on nubile naked flesh.

That went for blind men too, presumably, although Ortiz supposed they would require fertile imaginations to enjoy a night of blaring noise with nothing to observe onstage.

Most of his men were armed with compact submachine guns and pistols, though two had chosen shotguns sawed off fore and aft to measure just a fraction over two feet long. The SMG's and scatterguns were armpit-slung on leather harnesses, concealed beneath the coats of leisure suits in garish colors that turned nearly iridescent under El Gatito's flashing strobe lights. Pistols could be hidden anywhere—tucked under belts, in shoulder holsters, strapped to ankles—and the club's doormen made no attempt to scan potential boozers with metal-detecting wands.

Perfect.

If only they could find the strip club's owner, and the man they'd been assigned to kill, somewhere inside.

Ortiz was last in line to hand over his small admittance fee, letting his shooters enter well ahead of him. Inside, he scoped the clientele and had no difficulty spotting their intended target on the upper tier of the split-level party room. He looked enough like Pablo Escobar to pass a cursory inspection under blinding strobes, predictably surrounded by hulking security.

Half of El Tigre's men were too young to have seen the man they hunted on TV when he was still alive, but they had studied photographs at the hotel before departing for the Pussycat. Most of them had their mark spotted within their first few minutes in the club, and those who'd missed him were alerted by fellow *sicarios*. Ortiz had no need to direct them personally and, in fact, preferred the role of an observer to the action if that turned out to be possible.

If not, he was prepared to do or die for *Don* Joaquín.

Ortiz approached the bar, waiting his turn to order alcohol, not even caring what brands were available. Before one of the bartenders had time to serve him, his soldiers should have the VIP lounge zeroed in bring their target, with his gunmen and his flashy escorts, under fire.

Whatever happened after that was down to skill and fate.

While Ortiz stood in line, hoping the clubs sound system would be switched off when the shooting started, his eyes swept the club, checking for any hidden traps he might have missed so far. None were apparent, but he did see three *gringos,* two men flanking a woman, drifting toward the stairway leading to the mezzanine. They were not out of place per se—tourists were the lifeblood of Medellín's red-light district—but there was something odd about them all the same.

A moment later, Ortiz spied two more *gringos,* both men, moving in tandem toward a second flight of stairs that served the second-story space. El Tigre noted them particularly since they never once glanced at the dancing girls onstage, focused on Pablo Escobar or whoever in hell he was.

Ortiz flashed back to last night, at the laundromat and *llello* cutting plant, and froze. He broke that spell within a split-second, was reaching for the automatic in his shoulder holster, when the first shots echoed through the crowded space.

Natalie Karpin saw trouble approaching from a range of thirty yards, three young Latino men climbing the stairs to reach the VIP floor, reaching under suit coats as they climbed. Behind them and below, she glimpsed her fellow team members, Dartnell and Hardy, gaining on the stairs, which formed a mirror image of the steps she was ascending with the two Mahoney brothers.

And if there were other shooters in the club, approaching her intended target from that side, why wouldn't there be more on the staircase she occupied with Blake and Grant?

A backward glance informed here that there were, another trio, staring past her and her putative escorts, toward make-believe *Don* Pablo, his watchdogs and ladies of the evening. Nat saw a crossfire shaping up and for a heartbeat wondered how she should react: alert the brothers who ran SFX and hope they stood aside or kick the party off herself and see what happened next.

For Natalie, with innocent bystanders in the mix, it came down to no choice at all.

Turning to face the nearest three-man team, right hand inside her purse and going for her Glock, she warned Blake and his brother with a shout of "Guns!" One of the closest three Latinos took his eyes and mind off business long enough to spot her, see the weapon rising in her fist, and then the whole thing fell apart.

The shooter—maybe four or five years younger than Nat was, but with a hardened killer's eyes set in a baby face—revealed a cutdown shotgun, swinging it in her direction as he shouted something out in Spanish, warning his *amigos*. Karpin shot him in the throat, one round that caused a crimson jet to spurt out from his ruptured Adam's apple, dead or on his way before he toppled over backwards on the stairs.

His cohorts stepped away to either side, going for weapons of their own, as Karpin wondered how she'd flipped from being "Pablo's" would-be executioner to taking out a stranger with the same idea in mind.

Crazy.

She had no further time to think about it, as the other two *sicarios* produced machine pistols and brought them into play. Slightly above her on the stairs, Natalie felt rather than saw her two companions going into action, pistols in their hands. Away to Karpin's left as she faced toward the lewd display on stage, Dartnel and Hardy saw what was occurring and went for their carbon-copy Glocks, no safety levers to release thanks to the Austrian pistols' design.

And someone else was firing now, as well—not from steps leading up to the mezzanine, but from the lower floor. Nat just had time to sight more young Latinos angling weapons toward the VIP lounge when a loud alarm silenced the heavy metal music throbbing all around them.

Then the lights went out.

Reg Hardy dropped into a fighting crouch as someone switched off El Gatito's lights and sound system. Women— the dancers and a few customers dressed up to the nines— began to scream at once, while gunfire echoed through the room and muzzle flashes took the place of colored strobes.

Same shite, thought Hardy, *on another day.*

They'd walked into the middle of their third Medellín battle in the span of twenty hours, give or take. The former SAS man couldn't see a thing and held his fire, heard Dartnell cursing on the stairs until a backup generator came to life, illuminating ceiling-mounted flashlights at each corner of the party room.

Stupid, Reg thought, *to kill the barroom's lights when trouble starts, then have emergency lights switch on automatically in case of fire or some other calamity requiring swift evacuation.*

Which, in this case, meant a general stampede.

Above him, on the mezzanine, he heard men spitting curses in Spanish, the harsh metallic sound of weapons being primed for action. No one from the VIP section was firing yet, but others from the main floor and both stairwells were unloading, Natalie and the Mahoney brothers joining in across the way. Dartnell got off a single shot, angling toward where they'd last seen "Pablo" lounging with a babe on either side of him, cuddled against the guy who'd bought them for the night, but everyone was up and moving now, casting distorted shadows on the walls and ceiling painted in the likeness of a starry sky.

Chaos.

Their target's goon squad on the VIP floor had begun to fire at random, automatic weapons slinging death around the floor below, peppering walls, shattering liquor bottles on their shelves behind the bar. Hardy saw one dancer go down on stage, her legs in bloody tatters, just as "Pablo" and one of his escorts started running for an exit toward the second story's northeast corner.

"There!" he called to Stan Dartnell, while pointing toward the sprinters. "He's getting away.

"Like hell!" the Aussie answered back, firing a Glock round toward the two would-be escapees.

Stan missed "Escobar" but winged his backup man, taking him down ass-over-teakettle. They reached the point where he had fallen, kicked his Mini Uzi out of reach, and Hardy covered him while Dartnell trailed the main target across the mezzanine.

A moment later, Stan was back, cursing a blue streak, telling Reg, "I lost the bastard. They've got stairs down there, blacked out completely. Couldn't see a thing."

"We've got this wanker, anyway," Hardy replied. "Let's get him out of here."

Most of the VIP gunmen were down by now, or else had scattered in a search for cover, flipping over tables they could crouch behind. None of them seemed to notice as the two SFX men slugged their *compadre* into silence and began to drag him out of there, downstairs and back across the barroom slaughterhouse.

Now all they had to do was reach the street with him alive, collect the other members of their team, and haul ass out of there before *la policía* started to arrive in force.

Simple.

No worse than jumping off a cliff without a parachute.

El Tigre saw two white men running for an exit from the Pussycat, dragging a hunched Hispanic man between them who'd apparently been wounded in the VIP mezzanine lounge. He chased them with a double tap, knowing it was a waste of time and ammunition in the circumstances, and was proven right when they ducked through a door screened by a velvet curtain, vanishing from sight.

"*¡Los pinche gringos otra vez!*" he snarled.

Looked around for any of his men who might be near enough to send off in pursuit, he found none closer than thirty yards or so, converging on the upstairs lounge where their primary target had already disappeared. Whipping a compact wireless Blue Tooth from a pocket of his coat, Ortiz stuffed the earbud into place and keyed the microphone, commanding his *sicarios,* "Break off! We've missed him! Disengage!"

Most of them heard him, he was sure, but some were caught up fighting for their lives against their target's bodyguards or other gunmen pledged to keep the peace in El Gatito. It was far too late for that already, but while conscious of their failure, the defenders still felt honor-bound to risk their lives defending someone else's property.

Ortiz knew how that felt. He had been doing it himself since age fifteen, when he had killed his first man under orders from *Don* Joaquín Cardenas Sanchez at a whorehouse in Tlaquepaque, Jalisco. He had stabbed the man eleven times, thus earning both his nickname and promotion to the status of *sicario.*

He'd come a long way since that night, but death still dogged his tracks with every step.

And Ortiz did not plan on being killed for lack of shooting back.

A bullet whispered past his face and Ortiz spun to face the shooter—one of El Gatito's bartenders who'd grabbed a pistol from its place beside an ice machine. Before the slim *Colombiano* had a chance to try again, improve his aim, El Tigre shot him in the face and watched his left eye hurtle from its socket, sticking to the backbar mirror on impact. The dead or dying man collapsed, no longer visible behind the bar, and Ortiz started for the club's street exit.

"*¡Aclarar! ¡Hemos perdido nuestra oportunidad!*" he ordered through his Blue Tooth transmitter. *Clear out! We've missed our chance!*

El Tigre couldn't say how many of his soldiers heard or understood him, but the gunfire barely slackened as he neared the Pussycat's main doorway. There, another gunman waited, seeking targets, lining up on Ortiz as he glimpsed the weapon in El Tigre's hand.

They both fired simultaneously, as a fluke of timing brought one of the naked strippers in between them, hit from both sides on the run and screaming as she fell. That made the doorman hesitate, but his intended prey was made of sterner stuff.

Ortiz fired twice more, drilled holes in his adversary's chest, blood pumping from the entry wounds and the Colombian went down. Passing the body, Ortiz saw it twitching and took time to slash the dying soldier's left cheek open with a swift kick from one of his hand-tooled cowboy boots.

Take that, pendejo, thought El Tigre. *Come and find me later if you live.*

He trailed a human tide out through the street door, jostled through a milling huddle on the sidewalk, men and women both recoiling when he waved his pistol in their faces. Drunk or sober, they had seen enough of killing for one night and had no wish to join the victims scattered all around the inner rooms of El Gatito.

Ortiz had driven to the club alone, his men crammed five

apiece into three other rented cars. Reaching his vehicle, he slid behind the steering wheel and locked its four doors from inside, revving its engine as he glanced back toward the club.

How many of his men were still alive? How many had escaped without wounds that required a doctor's care?

El Tigre didn't know but trusted those alive and well to rendezvous at their hotel as soon as possible. Expecting to arrive before them, he rolled out, mind racing through the various parameters of having failed his merciless *padrone* a second time.

To miss his target twice was bad enough. Losing more men in the attempt, if any of them lay inside the strip club dead, only made failure that much worse. What had Cardenas said in closing their last conversation on the telephone?

You have another chance, Felipe, but it will be your last.

No more reprieves. Forgiveness only came from God, and El Tigre had parted company with Him for good, two decades earlier.

His only hope was to conceal the truth from *Don* Joaquín for now, regroup with any soldiers who'd survived the strike at El Gatito, and complete their mission as assigned. Final success might give his *jefe* pause, at least, before he sent a small army to take El Tigre down.

The cartel's structure was a rigid hierarchy, but it still left room for personal initiative, if those efforts produced desired results—and increased profits for *Don* Joaquín. From personal experience, El Tigre knew that it was usually easier to get forgiveness than permission.

But if he pressed on without authority and *failed*…well that could only mean a death reserved for traitors, slow and agonizing if Ortiz allowed himself to be captured alive.

Given the choice of certain death or possibly surviving, he would gladly roll the dice.

But if it came to death alone, by one means or another, El Tigre would choose the time and place.

Veredas Jalisco, Antioquia

Jorge Torrenegra, lately self-styled Pablo Escobar returned, had multiple hideouts around the city and department of his birth. The first Pablo was born in Rionegro, twenty-six miles southeast of Medellín, on the first day of December 1949 and died one day after his forty-fourth birthday in 1993. He'd never known the distant relative who would someday usurp his name and reputation, but Jorge liked to believe that Pablo would admire the sheer *machismo* or his effort to succeed.

But clearly not tonight.

For two nights in a row, attacks by disparate opponents—*gringos* piggybacking on another faction that might be Colombian, Bolivian, Peruvian or even Mexican—had forced him to accept setbacks and compelled him to conceal himself as Pablo had during his final days, a hunted fugitive.

His present hideout, in Veredas Jalisco, lay ten miles northwest of downtown Medellín. Abrupt departure from a night of dirty fun in Antioquia's capital had left his home in Los Colores momentarily unoccupied except for guards on duty, watching out for enemies around the clock. His latest bolt-hole, modest by the standards of a would-be Cocaine King, was situated eighty miles northwest of downtown Medellín, a long-abandoned factory he'd had refurbished into something more like home.

But it would never do, long-term.

Pablo/Jorge had his *sicarios* out searching high or low for any clue that might identify his latest enemies and let him rain down retribution on their heads. So far, the troops had disappointed him, and now—since the surprise attack on El Gatito—he was forced to cope without the sage advice of his lost second-in-command. He didn't know whether Gilberto Garavito was alive or dead after the strip club shootout, but his top lieutenant's failure to reach out, make contact, boded ill for both of them.

He hoped that Garavito, if already dead, had passed quickly and with a minimum of suffering. That wish was not mere sympathy, of course. If enemies had seized Gilberto without slaying him, it meant they would be grilling him for details about Torrenegra's operation, how and where to find the revenant of Pablo Escobar and bring his dreams of empire crashing down.

Gilberto Garavito was a hard man, true enough. But life had taught Jorge that no one—absolutely no one—could resist skillful interrogation in the long run. Every man and woman had a breaking point, whether evoked by drugs or hypnotism, primal pain or threats against their loved ones.

Garavito loved no one and had a high pain threshold, as he'd proved on more than one occasion, but selected reading on that subject had informed Jorge that only certain individuals afflicted with what doctors called congenital analgesia possessed complete immunity to pain, and that condition in itself had deadly drawbacks. Those afflicted with it would not feel a cut or burn unless they happened to observe the injury, even if assault upon their flesh turned out to be life threatening.

"*Maldita si lo haces, maldita si no lo haces,*" Jorge muttered to himself.

Damned if you do, damned if you don't.

"What's that, *jefe?*" asked Rafael Bernal, Jorge's third-in-command and natural successor to Gilberto Garavito if his number two was lost to him.

"*Nada.* What word from the patrols so far?"

"Nothing, *Señor.* They say that they are checking everywhere."

"You doubt then?" Torrenegra challenged him.

"No, *jefe.* I believe they are simply confused by these attacks."

As I am, Jorge thought, but kept it to himself.

He understood retaliation from the other cartel leaders he was pushing out of power and had planned for that. Whoever his Latino adversaries were, regardless of their nationality, he recognized their motives and their desperation to eliminate a major threat. He would identify them soon enough and strike directly at whoever sent them after him.

As for the *gringos*...they were unexpected, what American's called "wild cards" in a game of chance, and they had beaten him three times now. Who could he turn to for assistance when his sources in the underworld were blind?

Who else but someone well connected to the *pinche* DEA?

Le Candelaria, Medellín

Brigadier General Sandino stood amidst the wreckage of the El Gatito strip club, trying to ignore the officer beside him, who was carping over jurisdiction for the massacre. He was a captain with the Medellín Police Department, named Alfonso Teodoro, fifty-odd years old, with bushy eyebrows more impressive than his sparse mustache.

"I tell you, *General,*" he said, using Sandino's rank as if it were an insult rather than an honored title, "my department has responsibility for solving crimes like this within the city limits."

"Crimes like these," Sandino mused, his dark eyes scanning the destruction that surrounded them, "involve cartels of *narcotrafficantes* that are national and international in scope. That shifts investigation and solution to the National Police, and I command that agency in Antioquia."

"Perhaps," the captain granted. "But their victims here are local residents, which fall under my purview."

"So, you have identified them all, Captain?"

The lower-ranking officer could only frown at that. "Not all, so far, but most."

The wounded had been carted off to local hospitals. Those whose injuries were not life threatening were sent to the Clínica las Américas, while gravely wounded individuals rode ambulances to the Hospital Pablo Tobón Uribe, lights flashing and sirens wailing. Persons slightly injured, found with weapons on or near their persons, were confined to a secure ward at Hospital General de Medellín, each guarded by two officers, one from the local force, together with one of Sandino's men.

The dead, meanwhile, lay where they'd fallen, undisturbed beyond a cursory examination seeking signs of life. Those slain—some of them accidentally, Sandino thought—included two dancers, both nude but lightyears distant from attractive now, five patrons caught in the wrong place at the wrong time, and seven male combatants. None of those were carrying I.D., although Sandino recognized two men he'd seen in company with Jorge Torrenegra when they'd met on previous occasions.

Bodyguards who'd botched their last assignment and had paid the price in blood.

There were no *gringos* left behind, although one bartender claimed several had been involved in what transpired. He claimed one of them was a woman, though Sandino thought the witness's intelligence left much to be desired.

The captain's harping voice intruded on Sandino's

thoughts once more. "*Señor,* I must insist that you—"

"Insist to my superiors, Captain," Sandino interrupted him, "who easily outrank your own. Perhaps you should contact the General Director or his boss. I assume you know Carlos Trujillo Minister of National Defense?"

"Not personally, General, but—"

"Perhaps your own chief knows him, eh? Tell him that you insist on meddling in a national investigation. If you need a telephone I'll lend you mine."

As if in answer to his words, Sandino's cell phone chose that moment to distract him. He retrieved it, checked its screen, suppressed an urge to scowl at the announcement "PRIVATE CALL."

"*Perdóneme*, Captain," Sandino said, turning away. "This call is urgent."

Frowning as he turned his back on Teodoro, Raül Sandino took the call reluctantly. His phone might call it "private," but he didn't need three guesses to determine who was calling him.

"*Hola,*" he told the caller.

"We must meet," Medellín's premiere impostor said.

"I am at El Gatito now," Sandino said. "I can't just leave."

"How long, then?"

"I would guess at least an hour, maybe longer."

"Make haste," said Torrenegra. "Call when you are leaving there, and I'll direct you."

"When I can," Sandino answered back, but he was talking to dead air.

Arvi Regional Park Medellín

Parque Arvi lies nineteen miles northeast of downtown Medellín, a combined ecological nature preserve and pre-Hispanic archeological site on the eastern slopes of Aburrá Valley. It sprawls over four thousand acres, 10 percent of which remain natural forest, encompassing the suburbs of Bello, Envigado and Copacabana. It generates substantial revenue from ecotourism but still harbors secluded hideaways.

One such had been a hunting lodge until Colombia outlawed that blood sport back in February 2019, standing empty till the DEA acquired it on the cheap and turned it into a safe house for squealers ratting on the various cocaine cartels. It was unoccupied at present, thanks to Preston Chandler's intervention to assist the SFX team but still had electric power, running water, and revealed no sign of being breached by trespassers this night after the El Gatito firefight.

"Looks okay from here," said Blake Mahoney, as he helped Nat Karpin drag their captive from the backseat of their rented car. Dartnell and Hardy were responsible for bagging him, back at the Pussycat strip club, but Blake and Nat had taken custody once they had cleared the killing ground, driving him to the spot where Grant Mahoney had directed them.

The whole team was assembled when they dragged the prisoner inside and led him to a spacious kitchen where they had access to water, flame, and cutting implements. Duct tape secured the scowling *narcotrafficantes* to a straight-backed kitchen chair, its legs positioned far enough apart to keep the seat from tipping easily.

The team normally shied away from torture, both on grounds of principle and understanding that it seldom worked as planned. From U.S. occupation of the Philippines through Vietnam, on to Iraq's prison at Abu Ghraib, interrogators had discovered that a subject would say anything for a respite from pain, learning to read exactly what his captors wanted, feeding off tidbits of information they supplied. The CIA and U.S. Army's Military Intelligence Corps had wasted weeks, months, even years trying to verify a story they'd procured during "enhanced" interrogation, all in vain. Things went from bad to worse when spooks farmed out their dirty work to sadists in "black sites" maintained by "friendly" dictators around the world. In those cases, both victims and their torturers would often lie—the former for a moment of relief, the latter to keep cash flowing their way from Washington.

That said, it didn't mean the SFX team would not threaten pain or worse when necessary for a job's successful outcome and a payday for themselves. As for pursuing threats with action, that depended on the situation and their mood.

Grant didn't have to ask their prisoner his name. They knew that from the file and photographs supplied by Preston Chandler when they'd signed on for the work in Medellín. Before them sat Gilberto Garavito, second-in-command to their ultimate target. No one higher up in the resuscitated Medellín Cartel had yet been photographed by any agent of the DEA or FBI. If someone from the CIA had captured him on film or video, their headquarters at Langley in Virginia hadn't yet confessed as much.

That was a major problem with bureaucracy. The right hand often had no clue what the left hand was doing at a given time—nor was the poorly executed chaos limited to just two hands. Offhand, either Mahoney brother could have named sixteen distinct and separate agencies comprising the U.S. Intelligence Community, all overseen in theory by one director, chosen by the President. No less than ten discrete committees, boards councils supervised the operations of those factious, often mutually hostile cliques, ensuring that each agency's director placed a premium on keeping information classified and hoping agents in the field were working by the book.

The net result: confusion often bordering on chaos, and a windfall for those private military companies who slashed red tape and solved problems more expeditiously, without the internecine backstabbing.

When everyone was situated comfortably in the kitchen, save for Garavito taped and handcuffed to his chair, they settled down to business. Grant Mahoney stood before their captive, yanked away the silver tape had been serving Garavito as a gag.

"Okay," Mahoney told the prisoner. "We know your name and who you work for. I just have a few more questions. How it goes from here on out is up to you."

Granizal, Medellín

A smaller party of *sicarios,* none of them boastful now, had gathered in El Tigre's suite after the shootout in La Candelaria. Instead of fifteen men he'd started with originally, six of them replaced to cover losses from their first skirmish in Medellín, his total force was down to ten, counting himself and Isidro Buendia.

Nine against two hostile forces rather than the one he'd counted on, and Ortiz still had no idea who'd put the *pinche gringos* on his trail. And El Tigre's choice came down to quitting, facing execution for his failure, or pressing ahead without informing *Don* Cardenas of the latest setback.

No real choice at all.

He was about to pose that problem to his men and leave the final choice to them—those who prefer to die for quitting, raise your hands—when he was suddenly distracted by the muted buzzing of his cell phone.

"*¡Mierda!*"

Checking out his phone's LED screen before he took the call, Ortiz discovered that it was not *Don* Joaquín or anyone of his acquaintance from Jalisco. No, the call originated from a Medellín transmission tower, though the caller's name and a specific address were concealed.

Raising a hand for silence from his men, Ortiz said, "*¿Hola?*"

"*¿Hablas ingles, sí*" a voice he did not recognize inquired.

"I do," El Tigre said, and waited.

Switching languages, no accent that Ortiz could readily identify, the caller asked, "How would you like to get your hands on Pablo's second-in-command tonight?"

Frowning, Ortiz replied, "You have him?"

"No. But I can tell you where to find him and who's got him."

"While expecting what for such great generosity?"

"Take care of him however pleases you. If he can lead you back to Pablo, take 'em both out anyway you like. They've been a pain in my ass, same as yours and *Don* Joaquín's."

American, El Tigre thought, nearly convinced of it.

"A gift for nothing, then?"

"If you can use it, be my guest," the caller said. "I'll be in touch again, somewhere down range, and maybe your employer will decide to pay me what it's worth to him."

"A more suspicious man might think this is a trap," Ortiz replied.

"Just think about it. If I have your private number and can reach you anytime I want, why would I bother playing hide-and-seek to drop a net on you?"

"*Todo bien.* Where can I find him?"

"Do you have a pen and paper, *amigo?* I only plan to say this once."

Arvi Regional Park

Gilberto Garavito sneered at the strangers surrounding him, his facial grimace echoed in his voice.

"You think I'm gonna tell you something, *gringos,* eh?" He snorted out some version of a laugh. "That tells me that you don't know nothing about me, who I am or where I come from, what I've done."

"We've got a fair idea," said Blake Mahoney, "from the

trash you work for."

"You say 'trash'," their prisoner replied. "Ask anyone poor person in Antioquia what Pablo's done for them over the years. They worship him, *pendejo.*"

"Worship, right," Blake said. "How many gods can you name who have had their brains blown out?"

"It hasn't kept him down, though, eh?" Gilberto challenged. "Back he comes, as good as new. *Better* then new."

"Your hero's mastered death," Reg Hardy chimed in from the sidelines. "So, what made him duck out of the strip club? Wouldn't an immortal character stand up and fight? What's he afraid of?"

"Beating death don't make him no one's fool," the narcotrafficker replied. "He's smarter now than last time he was in this world."

"Can we cut through the voodoo shite?" Hardy asked no one in particular. "Let's get on with it, yeah?"

"Do whatever you want," Gilberto taunted them. "Get out your waterboard. If that's not good enough, I see knives hanging over there." The captive raised his head to indicate a nearby rack of cutlery some tenant of the former lodge had left behind.

"He's right," Grant said. "We may as well get started. It could take a while, tough monkey like this guy."

"We've got all night," Blake answered. Walking over to the knife rack, he took down a cleaver, wiped dust from its blade, and said, "Somebody want to get his shoes off? We can drop them at a thrift shop when we're done, since he won't need them anymore."

"You don't scare me, *gringo.* Can't show me anything I haven't seen or done before. Come on and hack away!"

"Like that old YV program used to say," Blake answered back. "You asked for it."

Gilberto's ankles were secured with duct tape to the chair's front legs. When Stan Dartnell knelt down to pull his shoes off, Garavito couldn't kick or otherwise resist.

"I'll leave the socks," Stan said. "They might soak up some of the blood."

"Big man," their captive sneered at Blake. "You let me go, we'll see who winds up with that cleaver in his head."

"You need to pay attention," said the SFX vice president. "The show isn't *Let's Make a Deal*."

"It might as well be *Chinga to Madre*," Gilberto sneered, then spat at Dartnell.

Stan responded with a hard right to the gut that emptied Garavito's stomach of the last few drinks he'd tossed down at the Pussycat.

"No table manners, this one," said Natalie Karpin.

"Spoiled his pants," Stan said. "And they were only ten or twelve years out of style." Rising, he tossed the shoes aside and turned to Blake. "Okay. All yours."

Maybe it was a bluff, and maybe not. Their time was short and getting shorter by the minute. Either way, they never got a chance to test that proposition.

When the front wall of the one-time hunting lodge imploded, shattered bricks and strips of mutilated lumber flew across the parlor, some bits of the shrapnel going farther, rattling on the kitchen floor and counters. In the aftermath of that blast, everyone could smell the reek of octogen or HMX, a powerful nitroamine high explosive, chemically akin to RDX, together with the scent of melted wax that made up 5 percent of standard Russian RPG warheads.

By that time, all five of the SFX commandos had found cover, priming weapons in reaction to the sneak attack. The team rushed to confront invaders, firing short bursts from their AK-9 carbines at dodging shadow-figures, ducking the return fire until their adversaries sprinted toward a pair of SUVs and roared off into darkness without turning on their headlights. Brake lights still invited fire until the boxy vehicles were out of sight and screened by trees along the former hunting lodge's one-lane access road.

"Is anybody hit?" Grant asked his team.

The other four were all unscathed except for minor scraped and bruises suffered during the initial blast, ready to follow their attackers if Mahoney gave the word.

Instead, he cautioned them, "We'd better see to Garavito or he'll try to work free from the tape."

Or not, as it turned out.

Returning to the kitchen, Blake Mahoney saw it first and said, "Well, shit!"

One of the front wall's bricks—or half of one—had scored a bullseye on the *llello* smuggler's forehead, punching through the bone between his eyebrows and hairline, jutting outward like the horn on a Ray Harryhausen movie cyclops from the latter 1950s. Blood streamed down his face from the horrendous wound, his open eyes already glazed in death.

"He won't be talking now," Natalie said, stating the obvious.

"Unless he said, 'Hello' to Satan on his way downstairs," Reg Hardy said.

"I didn't know you were religious," Dartnell quipped.

"I'm not," Hardy replied. "I just take comfort from the thought of scum like this guy roasting for eternity."

"Whatever gets you through the night, mate."

"Right back at you," Hardy said.

"Should we just leave him here?" asked Natalie.

"He's no more use to us," Blake said.

"One thing we need to think about, though," brother Grant chimed in.

"How did whoever blasted him know where to find him?" Blake replied.

"And more importantly, how to find *us*," Grant answered back.

12

Click Clack Hotel

The SFX team hadn't wasted much time sweeping the ex-hunting lodge to clear forensic evidence. They'd wiped the unused cleaver down for fingerprints and left Gilberto Garavito lying where'd he'd fallen; otherwise, they left the building's dust and disarray, together with the aftermath of battle, to confuse authorities when they eventually happened on the scene.

That might be soon or weeks away, depending on what else distracted the National Police in their perpetual investigation of "subversives" who might range from active terrorists to labor organizers or the unemployed who dared to raise a voice against the ruling Democratic Center Party. Grant Mahoney knew the DRP's motto was "Strong Hand, Big Heart," but the strong hand always seemed to dominate given the nation's history since World War II—except, of course, when it came down to wiping out the drug cartels.

As for the National Police, they had a mixed record at best. Its first training academy had not been organized till 1964, and even then its stated purpose was "indoctrination" of majors and lieutenant colonels. Lower ranks, mostly ex-soldiers, got along as best they could, while higher-ranking officers were hand-picked for their service to the DRP.

"Improvements" had been certified from Washington during the 1990s, after Pablo Escobar went down—assuming that he had, in fact—but a wiretapping scandal rocked the agency during 2007 and complaints of brutality against peaceful protesters had rated notice by Human Rights Watch in 2019.

Sometimes, the more things change, the more they stay the same.

Back at the Click Clack, while his team tried to relax and ordered food up to their rooms, Grant used his cell to contact Preston Chandler at the DEA. It was long after hours for their contact to be at his desk, but Chandler's hours were irregular by definition. When he answered on the second ring, he sounded wide-awake and clear of mind.

"What have you got for me?" he asked.

"Less than I'd like," Grant said. "We caught a glimpse of Pablo, as they call him, but he slipped away from us."

"And now he's in the wind?"

"I doubt that he'll go far. For what it's worth, we bagged his number one lieutenant based on information from your man down here."

"Camilo?"

"Right. Bad news about him, I'm afraid," Grant said.

"I'm listening." The DEA man's voice was wary now.

"He wasn't taking calls, so I had people go to the apartment address he supplied. The cops and coroner were there ahead of us."

A moment's silence on the line, then Chandler said, "That is bad news. Of course, he understood the risks that he was taking in return for various rewards."

Grant didn't have to ask what those were, not that Chandler would admit giving one narcotrafficker a virtual free hand for serving others to him on a plate.

Filling the momentary silence, Grant said, "Given his double-dealing, I can't speculate on who might want him dead right now, but the coincidence of timing doesn't track for me."

"No. I don't like it either," Chandler granted. "What's the word on Garavito? Is he talking to you? I imagine cracking him would take some time and effort."

"We ran out of time," Mahoney said. "Somebody dropped a dime on where we'd taken him—don't ask me how, yet—and they crashed the party. When the smoke cleared, Garavito was in no shape to say anything."

"Jesus! And your people?"

"They're fine, so far. No thanks to whoever's been running parallel to us and hunting Pablo."

"Any fix on who they might be?"

"Nothing solid," Grant replied. "Hispanic, but that could mean any group he's irritated lately, from Colombia up to Tijuana, maybe even Ciudad Juárez."

Aside from prospects close to home, plus rivals in Peru and in Bolivia, Grant knew that Mexico harbored at least a dozen rival drug cartels, participants in the ongoing drug wars that had claimed so many lives since Christmas of 2006. While no two sources commonly agreed, reports syndicate-related homicide from both sides of the Tex-Mex border ranged above 160,000 with no end in sight.

"I'll see what I can find out," Chandler said, "and call you back."

"Appreciate it."

"In the meantime, there's one place that I can think of where our guy might go to ground. Are you familiar with Veredas Jalisco?"

"I won't have any problem finding it," Mahoney said.

"Northwest of Medellín. A decent map should tell you more. Word has it that he's got a place there, where he goes to duck the heat from time to time."

"Address?"

"I've got one for you, but it's unconfirmed officially.

You have something to write with?"

"Go ahead," Mahoney answered, trusting in his memory.

Chandler delayed another moment, maybe paging through a file or notebook wherever he was, then read a street address of Via a San Pedro de las Milagros.

Grant knew "*milagros*" was the Spanish word for "miracles." Toss in a saint's name and he understood the highway's designation to be one of countless devoted to religion that repeated everywhere New Spain had once held sway.

"Got it," he said, the maybe address for his target stored away in mind.

"Okay, then," Chandler said. "I'll wish you better luck, then, and start rattling some cages up this way."

"More later," said Mahoney, then hung up without superfluous goodbyes.

He'd give the team some time to finish up their meals, then gather them for what he hoped might be the final briefing on their job in Medellín.

Hoping it wouldn't be the last time some of them took to the field.

El Poblado, Medellín

El Tigre heard his cell phone buzz and reached for it, checking the ornate sunburst wall clock in his suite at the Stanza Hotel. He frowned, confirming that it was an hour earlier where *Don* Joaquín Cardenas lived, and even now, in later middle age, his *jefe* rarely went to bed before the break of day.

Ortiz checked out his phone and saw the legend "UNKNOWN CALLER, NUMBER BLOCKED." That would not be Cardenas, even with calling through a scrambler to prevent eavesdroppers from recording a coherent conversation. Nor should it be any of his men, whether relaxing in their rooms or downstairs in the lounge, maybe trolling the rooftop bar for female company.

He took the call. "*¿Hola?*"

"How badly do you want to stay alive?" an unfamiliar man's voice asked.

"*¿Quien es este?*" El Tigre demanded.

"Never mind who this is. Do you want to stay alive and please your boss, or wind up like the soldiers you've already lost?"

Ortiz let that pass, knowing that any answer he might give would be incriminating. For all he knew, someone could be taping every word that passed over the line.

Switching to English, he informed the caller, "You must have the wrong number, *Señor.*"

"Okay, play it that way," the caller said. "It wouldn't be the first mistake I ever made. But just in case I'm talking to Felipe Ortiz, working for *Don* Joaquín Cardenas Sanchez, listen up. I won't repeat myself."

That time, Ortiz let silence be his answer.

"Good," the stranger said. "I understand you're hunting for a ghost and getting nowhere. Maybe you should check out this address. Ready?"

El Tigre still made no reply.

"I'll take that as a yes," his caller said, the smirk in his voice readily apparent. Next, he read an address, then repeated it before he signed off with, "I hope you got that, Tiger. Happy hunting."

Ortiz listened to the dial tone for a second, then the red telephone icon to end the call. He sat, mind racing, working through the angles of the unexpected call.

It had to be a trap, of course—but what if it was not?

Who was the stranger, seemingly a *gringo,* who appeared to know so much about El Tigre's recent trials in Medellín? How did the caller know Ortiz, much less his mission in Colombia? And why the offer of assistance now, assuming it was not a trap?

Ortiz never suspected that Cardenas was behind the call. His *padrino* was a sly man, demonstrated by survival to his present age, but he did not play childish games. If *Don* Joaquín knew where to find the man posing as Pablo Escobar, he would have sent El Tigre's team directly there to finish it.

No. This was someone else, acting from motive that El Tigre could not fathom yet.

But he could not afford to sit back and ignore the lead, either.

Anticipating treachery and mortal danger, he still had to check it out, see if his quarry might indeed be found at the location specified. He and his men would take the risk, but with the utmost caution, on alert for any chance the call was fake, meant to betray them.

What El Tigre would not—*could* not—do was call Guadalajara with the latest news. It was too thin, and if it blew up on his face, Ortiz would rather die without his last message from *Don* Cardenas being words of mockery and scorn.

Better to die trying than be recalled and stand before a failure's firing squad.

Scowling, El Tigre raised his cell phone and began to rally his *sicarios.*

Click Clack Hotel

The SFX team was assembled once again in Grant Mahoney's suite. He briefed them on his latest talk with Preston Chandler, then fielded the questions he'd expected from the others.

"How'd he take the news of his informant being taken out?" Blake asked.

"In stride, I'd say," Mahoney told his younger brother. "Román won't have been the first stoolie he's lost who played both ends against the middle."

"Not surprised, though?" Hardy asked.

"Took it in stride, I'd say. The level where he operates,

losses are factored in."

"About this address, mate," said Stan Dartnell. "I have to wonder why he didn't give it to us earlier."

"I didn't ask him," Grant replied. "But if I had to guess, I'd say he had his fingers crossed that we could lay this so-called ghost to rest before he had to reel off everyplace the guy was ever spotted."

"So, we're going in?" asked Natalie.

"After we scout the place," Grant said.

"You trust Chandler that far, bro?" Blake inquired.

Grant answered with a lazy shrug. "It's worth a look, I'd say. We don't commit unless it's doable and we spot something to confirm our man is actually on the scene."

"I'll scope it for you, right enough," Hardy put in. "But it could take some time. I can't be everywhere at once."

"Do what you can. We'll all have field glasses, besides your optics," Grant replied.

Stan Dartnell spoke next. "Assume this Pablo Escobar, or whoever in hell he is, is hiding out like anybody else would after what went down at El Gatito, he won't just be strolling in the open, taking the night air. He'll be locked down and out of sight behind an army of *sicarios*."

"Most likely," Grant agreed.

"And math was never my best subject," Stan pressed on. "But I can count our team on one hand, Chief."

"We've kicked their asses three times so far," Grant said.

"With help from some Latino mob that's gunning for the same man we are," Natalie reminded him. "And even so, we haven't gained much from it. So far, we've got one dead hostage and one dead informant who was likely feeding us a line of *bupkis* anyway."

"But Chandler's still alive," Blake interjected. "Would he contract for two mill, with half up front, to set us up? Does that make any sense?"

Playing the Devil's advocate, Grant said, "I'm still working on that. Until we have an answer locked down tight, let's call the next move 'search.' We'll save 'destroy' for what we find and how it plays out down the line."

"Sounds fair enough to me," Hardy agreed. "As long as we go in with exit strategies in mind."

"We always do," Grant said.

"Sticking out heads into the lion's mouth," Dartnell opined. "Or I suppose it should be jaguar's mouth, considering we're in Colombia."

"Two things to bear in mind," Grant told the team. "First, if we scrub the job, we'll have to give Chandler his million dollars back and eat expenses. Second, if this Pablo lookalike is anywhere near close to pulling off his plan, rebuilding Escobar's empire and possibly expanding it, somebody needs to take him out as soon as possible."

"So, our next move is…what?" inquired Dartnell.

"Split up and see to your equipment. Lock and load. Dress for success. We roll in thirty minutes for short road trip. Be extra careful going into the approach, safe distance from the property, and close the gap on foot."

"I hope this isn't one big-ass mistake," the Aussie said, sounding resigned.

"You and me both," Grant answered him, repeating it for emphasis. "You and me both."

They had a job to do, granted, but Grant Mahoney's team was still his first concern. They trusted him rather than any given client who employed them. It was down to him, vetting the task, arranging preparations for a reasonable option of success, getting them in and out again. Each member of the consortium was independent and supremely competent in his or her own right, but each of them was only human after all. They could be wounded, killed, in seconds flat on any mission they agreed to overtake.

And whose fault would it be for choosing the wrong client, the wrong job, the wrong location to attempt it against the wrong odds?

All mine, Grant thought, while putting on a smile that radiated confidence he didn't feel.

Veredas Jalisco, Antioquia

Reinforcements kept arriving at the Torrenegra property in twos and threes, with several larger parties, as the night wore on. All brought a complement of arms and ammunition with them, stocking up the arsenal they felt might be required to shield their supernatural *padrino* from his lurking enemies.

The man in charge, meanwhile—whatever name might be applied to him at any given moment—still had no clear-cut idea of who those enemies might be.

A spy working on his behalf in Mexico, specifically in Guadalajara, suspected that *Don* Joaquín Cardenas Sanchez was to blame for some of the attacks, and that made sense to Jorge Torrenegra. His cartel had cut into the *Mexicano's* business during recent months, and "Pablo," as his people knew him, knew that the invasion would not pass without a violent response. Granted, the recent raids upon his *llello* cutting plant, his trucks and El Gatito still had managed to surprise him, but invaders from Jalisco did not solve the mystery entirely.

Torrenegra knew *Don* Joaquín's methods, understood that while he sometimes entered into dealings with the CIA, he'd never hired a *gringo* gunman in his life, much less a team of four or five on which a woman was included.

No.

That aspect of the threat to Torrenegra's growing empire emanated from some other source, and he would not be safe until he managed to identify and liquidate that enemy, wherever he was based.

"Pablo" reborn was watching two of his *sicarios* set up a special weapon they had managed to acquire from some black-market source for this special occasion. It was a K3 light machine gun manufactured by Daewoo Precision Industries in Busan, South Korea. Some four hundred of them had been purchased by the Military Forces of Colombia back in 2006, for use against insurgent guerrillas supporting the Revolutionary Armed Forces of Colombia (FARC) and its rival National Liberation Army (ELN), and this one was presumably pilfered from some army warehouse or other since then.

The K3 outwardly resembled both the U.S.-made M60 and the Belgian FN Minimi machine guns. Like those latter weapons, it was chambered for 5.56×45mm NATO rounds, but would also handle .223 Remington ammunition, spitting bullets from either at seven hundred rounds per minute when belt-fed, accelerating to one thousand per minute when armed with a box magazine. Its effective range was advertised as 875 yards, its hypothetical maximum pegged at roughly 2,900.

In skilled hands, Torregegra thought, it should stop anyone who tried to kill him at his hideaway.

His cell phone, buzzing from its pouch on Torrenegra's hand-tooled belt, distracted him. He checked its screen and saw the cryptic logo "BGS." Frowning, he drew the phone out of its sheath and took the call.

"*Buena noches*, Brigadier."

"No names!" Raül Sandino cautioned him.

"My telephone's secure," Jorge assured the general. "Is yours?"

"We cannot be too careful."

"So, why are you calling me?"

"My men have found your missing *teniente*. I regret to tell you he is dead."

Jorge detected no trace of regret in Brigadier Sandino's tone but understood that nothing would be gained by calling him a bald-faced liar.

"When and where?" he asked instead.

"At an abandoned hunting lodge in Parque Arvi. It appears that he was taken there from El Gatito earlier."

"*¿Los gringos?*"

"Not unless they bound him to a chair, as if to question him, then went outside and fired a rocket at the lodge to kill him," said Sandino. "*No tiene sentido.*"

Indeed, it made no sense. "What are you saying, then?" asked Torrenegra.

"Whoever kidnapped Garavito took him to the park, most likely planning to interrogate him and discover where to find you. *Alguien más* arrived and took them by surprise, killing your man either by accident or in an effort to annihilate all those inside the lodge."

"What do you mean by 'someone else'?" demanded Torrenegra.

"It's a pity that I cannot say," the brigadier replied. "After the rocket blast—a Russian RPG, my people think, sold by the millions everywhere—a firefight followed. We found brass inside the lodge and out from various Kalashnikov weapons. Inside were 9×39mm cartridges. Outside, the raiders fired 7.62×39mm."

"And no one else was hit?" asked Torrenegra, trying to imagine the confusion and its outcome.

"It appears not," Sandino replied. "Technicians are still working at the scene, but they report finding no blood except your *teniente*'s, from a head wound where a flying brick—"

"*¡Suficiente!*" Torrenegra cut him off. "Enough! If you have nothing else worthwhile to tell me—"

"Only that the killers traced your man and his abductors by some means as yet unknown to me. It seems they were directed to the lodge, likely the last place anybody would have looked for him. In which case…"

"*Sí.*" Jorge saw where the brigadier was going with that

line of reasoning. "If they could find him there, I must assume that they can find me here."

"You still have options if they have not reached you yet," Sandino said.

"To run away and hide, hoping they just give up? No, General. I've come too far and risked too much. If they come here, it will turn out to be the worst mistake they ever made."

"Good fortune to you, then. Officially, you understand, I can't appear to take your side."

"It makes me wonder what I pay you for, Raül."

"I've helped you often in the past and shall again," the brigadier replied, sounding annoyed. "If I'm exposed and sent to prison, then you've wasted all those pesos anyway."

Jorge made no response to that. He was remembering how his ancestor, whose identity he he'd claimed, had dealt with lawmen, prosecutors, even presidential candidates who had defied him. Most of them were dead now, fading memories, along with their extended families.

"For now, at least, it seems that we have nothing more to say." Before Sandino had a chance to answer, Torrenegra cut the link between them and returned his cell phone to its belt pouch.

A glance around the patio where his men tinkered with the K3 light machine gun found Rafael Bernal observing them. Jorge called out his name and beckoned, Bernal hastening to stand before him.

"¿Qué es, jefe? Anything you need…"

In clipped tones, Torrenegra briefed Bernal on Garavito's fate, providing no details. "You are promoted, Rafael," he said. "My second-in-command."

The young *sicario* beamed like a child on Christmas morning, opening a gift that he has craved all year. "¡Mil gracias padrino! I shall serve you well and never let you down."

"You may be called upon to prove that soon enough," Jorge replied.

13

Veredas Jalisco, Antioquia

Grant Mahoney had reviewed maps of their target in advance, selecting points where members of his team could park their rented vehicles in relative concealment and security. From those positions they hiked to a central rally point two hundred yards from the site where Preston Chandler claimed their man had gone to ground after the El Gatito raid.

When they were all assembled, laden down with firearms, ammunition, frag grenades and combat knives, Grant double-checked their preparation for the strike that could be all or nothing, do or die.

One thing about the Internet that soldiers of another generation had been forced to do without was Google Earth. Some keyboard typing and a mouse-click could present multiple photographs of nearly anyplace around the world, including shots taken from satellites on high to street views capturing the entrances to private driveways, fences and the like. Granted, the photos weren't presented in real time—a car awaiting entry at a given gate might have arrived last week or moments earlier, for instance—but smart money said the layout of a chosen property had not been changes significantly since the last flyover.

"Pablo Escobar's" hideout at Veredas Jalisco sat on twelve or thirteen acres, wooded for the most part and surrounded by a brick retaining wall approximately nine feet high, with broken glass set into concrete at its pinnacle. The only gate for entering or exiting the property was manned by armed guards, but they had apparently dispensed with dogs. The main house was L-shaped and looked to be two stories tall, with two chimneys, a dish antenna, and a backyard mast apparently designed for transmitting signals via cell phones and/or radio. There was a pool in back, approximately half Olympic size, and a veranda with a large brick barbecue. No outdoor sports facilities were visible, but Grant supposed that after beating death, "Pablo" had lost his taste for soccer and for racing motorcycles.

Maybe he had simply gotten tired.

Standing in near darkness, clouds mostly covering a quarter moon, Grant finished running down the final checklist one last time. Reg Hardy had picked out a Spanish lime tree, sixty-odd feet tall, that overlooked their target from the northwest, giving him a vantage point from which to scan the layout with the PSO-1 telescopic sight mounted atop his OTs-03 SVU sniper rifle, ready to advise his teammates on the movements of their enemies or intervene if need be to defend them.

Entering the walled-off property would be a dicey proposition, but the team's remaining four commandos—the Mahoney brothers paired, while Stan Dartnell and Nat Karpin went in together—each had scaling gear including nylon rope, a grappling hook, and armored leather gantlets that, with any luck at all, would let them clear the jagged glass topping the wall at points where they planned scrambling from the outside in.

And once inside, they would be on their own, outnumbered and outgunned.

As Helmuth von Moltke, a German general from the 19th Century once said, "No battle plan survives first contact with the enemy."

But going in without a plan at all was tantamount to suicide.

Dartnell and Karpin would be climbing over from the north, while Grant and Blake Mahoney scaled the southwest corner of the outer wall. Whatever happened after that…well, that was anybody's guess.

El Tigre's strike force had been whittled down by losses from the raid on El Gatito earlier that night. One of his men was also operating with a bandaged scalp from their engagement with the *gringo* kidnappers at Avri Park—black cloth secured with electrician's tape to keep from making him a special target by moonlight on their approach.

That said, Ortiz planned on attacking in full force, which was to say nine men besides himself. En route to Veredas Jalisco, they had come upon a laundry truck and hijacked it, leaving the driver's body in a dumpster with his throat cut, bleeding out. El Tigre hoped that they could use the vehicle to crash the gate of "Pablo Escobar's" estate, or at the very least derail it so that Ortiz and his men could slip inside on foot.

It wasn't much, in terms of strategy, but El Tigre could manage nothing better in the rush from El Poblado following the nameless caller's tip to where their adversary might be found—with emphasis on "might be."

Without knowing who had called him, or how the anonymous caller had known that he existed at all, Ortiz had no way to evaluate the lead. He could not spare the time to check it out, so far from home, where he had no contacts with the police, telephone companies, or any other useful source.

The one thing he could *not* afford to do was sit by idly, wasting time, if there was any chance at all for him to deal with

"Escobar" as ordered by his master. Should he fail, it meant his last hope was exhausted and he might as well die here, shot down while trying to obey his orders than slink home and spend his last few days screaming for mercy in a dungeon.

But if he managed to succeed against the odds…

Then all would be forgiven, he would doubtless be rewarded, probably promoted to mid-level management, granted a small share of the cartel's monthly earnings off the top. In short, El Tigre would be set for life or whatever remained of it in the profession he had chosen for himself.

Each member of the team had checked and doublechecked his weapons, ammunition magazines, and any other gear he planned on carrying to battle with their enemies. Isidro Buendia was handling the RPG-7 grenade launcher, Guillermo Serradilla lugging the remainder of their 40mm high-explosive rounds. The rest were clinging to their AKS-74U automatic carbines, weighted down with bandoleers of extra magazines, pistols holstered in shoulder rigs or on their belts.

Whatever else they carried would be useful only during hand-to-hand combat, and thus likely superfluous. If it came down to knives, garottes and saps, their cause was lost.

Three miles remained until they reached the property his unknown caller had insisted was the hiding place of "Pablo Escobar," whoever he turned out to be in fact. At this point, Ortiz scarcely even cared. He'd glimpsed the man during the raid on El Gatito and would recognize him when they met again. The actor—as Ortiz believed he must be, although likely a demented one—resembled Escobar sufficiently to pass with people who had never met the real King of Cocaine before his death, but younger somehow, which made even less sense to El Tigre than a bullet-riddled man returning from the grave.

Was he supposed to be immortal *and* the owner of a time machine?

¡Ridículo!

Since no such things were possible, it had to be a fraud, but one backed up by government connections, military hardware, and an army of *sicarios*. Such things were difficult to overcome, even assuming that the man behind them was a charlatan.

"*Dos millas, jefe,*" said El Tigre's driver, Julio Benítez.

Two miles. Almost there. El Tigre keyed his walkie talkie, speaking to the wheelman in the stolen truck preceding Ortiz in his rented car. "Be ready for the gate approaching on your right, Alfredo," he ordered.

"*Sí, jefe,*" acknowledgement came back to him.

El Tigre clutched his Russian carbine tightly, index finger just outside its trigger guard for safety's sake. He saw the wall now, running long and straight along the road fronting his adversary's property, and up ahead the wrought-iron gate they must crash through to get inside.

The battle would be joined in seconds now.

Ortiz tried to prepare himself for anything, knowing that it was all in vain.

Ahead of him, the laundry truck swung toward the gate, accelerating as it strained for ramming speed. El Tigre braced himself, cursing nonstop as Julio Benítez followed closely in the leader's wake.

Reg Hardy saw the caravan approaching and alerted his teammates via his Blue Tooth microphone. He wasn't sure about the boxy truck in front until its driver swung off-road and powered toward the wrought-iron gate with grinding, clashing gears.

The guards on duty there, alarmed, were firing at the van with automatic weapons as it smashed into the gate and forced it into the runner set in concrete, twisting it, shoving the gate aside. The laundry truck surged forward, bright scars in its faded paint etched down the driver's side, taking repeated hits at point-blank range.

The gate struck one guard, sent him sprawling backward, while the other ducked and dodged, still firing at his enemies. Hardy had to decide whether he'd help the new arrivals or impede them, whichever might help his teammates as they scaled the wall surrounding "Escobar's" estate, and finally decided that it would hurt less to have two hostile factions fighting on the grounds than one intent solely on cutting down his friends.

Accordingly, he framed the second gate guard in the crosshairs of his telescopic sight and stroked his rifle's trigger, trusting its sound suppressor to disguise his sniper's nest. Down range, the human target's skull exploded, momentarily enveloped by a blood-red halo as the young *sicario* went down.

The dead guy's partner, swatted sprawling by the gate a moment earlier, was on his feet and firing at the crash truck now, ignoring what had happened to his sidekick. Hardy was about to drop him when the second carload of invaders swept in past the crumpled gate, an automatic carbine spitting from the backseat on its driver's side. Those slugs ripped through the second guard, punching him through a jerky little dance before his legs gave out and dumped him in a lifeless, leaking heap.

Two more vehicles followed through the gate, both scraping wrought iron as they passed but meeting no more opposition right away. Reg Hardy tracked the last one through the opening and saw a rubber-necking gunman peering through the dark sedan's rear window, making sure the coast was clear.

Another twitch of Hardy's trigger finger, and his OTs-03 SVU's next round drilled neatly through the tinted window glass, punching the gunman's face backward and out of frame before the car sped off toward "Pablo's" manor house.

Three soldiers down so far, out of how many on the grounds?

Reg didn't know and couldn't estimate how many new arrivals still survived inside the raider's caravan. His team-mates would be fighting for their lives in seconds flat, he realized. Was he more useful to them in his sniper's nest or on the ground, sharing their risk?

Deciding, Hardy cursed under his breath and started scrambling down the tree trunk in a rush.

"Pablo Escobar," born Jorge Torrenegra, clutched an MP5K submachine gun, shouting at his soldiers to advance and meet their enemies.

"*¡Date prisa, malditos imbéciles! ¡Mátalos!*"

If they heard him, none acknowledged the profane tirade, already forming up a ragged skirmish line and moving out to stop the convoy of invaders who had smashed his gate aside to charge the house. Beside him, carrying an M4 carbine with an M203 grenade launcher mounted underneath its barrel, Isidro Buendia told him, "I can stop the van, *jefe.*"

"Prove it, *amigo*!" Torrenegra snapped.

Buendia took two paces forward, raised the carbine to his shoulder, peering through its Aimpoint red-dot sight, his left hand wrapped around the M203 launcher's stubby pistol grip, index finger inside its trigger guard. The launcher was a single-shot weapon, breech-loaded, feeding 40mm rounds. When Buendia squeezed off, the launcher made a popping sound, the carbine's recoil jolting him.

Down range, the high-explosive canister impacted on the van's grill, less than two feet underneath its broad windshield, and detonated in a blaze of fire, immediately followed by a smoke cloud. Torrenegra didn't see the windshield buckle under pressure from the blast, but then the van lurched forward, stalling out, and he could see two bloody figures slumped in its front seat.

As Isidro grappled to reload his launcher, Torrenegra

watched the battle joined on his front lawn, *sicarios* unloading on the string of vehicles now stalled behind the laundry van. At the same time, he recognized that someone else was firing from behind his men, two weapons off to Torrenegra's left and two more on his right.

Now, what in the hell?

Given the general confusion and his distance from the action, Torrenegra could not have identified the four stray shooters by their looks. All four were dressed in black, three of them clearly male, but he couldn't be sure about the fourth, with longer dark hair tied back in a ponytail that might be unisex or indicate a woman dropped into the mix.

As at the laundromat last night, and then during the El Gatito raid?

Gringos!

It struck him then that things were going horribly, perhaps irrevocably wrong tonight. And with that thought, he understood that there might only be one option still remaining that would let him live to see another sunrise over Medellín.

"Isidro, have you seen Édgar Matiz?" he asked.

Matiz was the chief pilot of the Bell 525 Relentless helicopter sitting parked on the grass in back of Torrenegra's house, waiting to carry him away in an emergency.

"No, *jefe*," said Buendia. "Shall I go and find him?"

"We'll go together," Torrenegra said. "I think it's time we leave this place."

Natalie Karpin tried to keep an optimistic attitude, but in the present circumstances she was forced to wonder if the team had bitten off too much for it to chew, much less swallow.

She estimated there were forty soldiers on the grounds, at least, together with a dozen occupants or so of vehicles that had crashed through the gate, engaging "Escobar's" defenders in close-quarters battle. So far, she had dropped two men herself with short bursts from her AK-9 carbine, and Stan Dartnell was up to three, but they were still badly outnumbered and outgunned.

And what of that?

Her mind flashed back to other times when she had battled against longer odds—Syrian regulars, guerrillas in the Beqaa Valley fighting to defend their poppy fields—remembering that she'd survived on those occasions thanks to firepower and sheer determination to succeed.

Those helped, of course, but on the front lines of a war zone, one could only stretch her luck so far.

When an explosion rocked the van leading the short line of invaders' vehicles, both Natalie and Stan ducked low while shrapnel whined overhead. The van's back doors flew open, and a young man toting a Kalashnikov assault rifle sprang out, dodging the second car in line that nearly sandwiched him against the stalled-out, smoking van.

He turned toward Nat and Stan, seemed startled to confront a woman on the killing ground, but he recovered swiftly, hoisting his AK to cut loose from the hip. Both SFX commandos fired on him at the same time, stitching a neat half-dozen holes across his chest and abdomen, punching him over on his back. He struck the chase car's left-front fender, bounced back from it, and collapsed onto his face.

By that time, everybody on the grounds was firing, some at enemies they'd singled out, others apparently to make themselves feel useful in the swirl of combat's chaos. Natalie broke to the left, in the direction of their target's house, unsure whether Stan was following her lead, not taking time to check and see. With enemies running and shooting all around them, calling out for him to stick with her felt like a waste of time and breath.

She started for the main house on her own, imagined

that she'd glimpsed their foremost target on the porch, but they a bullet whispered past her face, making her duck, and when she glanced up at the manor's porch again whoever she had seen was gone, most likely ducking back inside.

The only way to check it out was by advancing, getting closer, hoping she could make her way inside.

"*¡Gringa!*"

The shout behind her made Natalie turn, facing a slim *sicario* a few years younger than her twenty-nine years if his face was any indicator. He was leveling an Uzi sub-machine gun at her but had called her out instead of firing instantly. That proved to be the worst mistake of his short life as Natalie squeezed of a short burst from her AK-9 before he could react, her bullets drilling through his lungs and heart from right to left.

The impact tossed him over backwards, sprawling on the driveway's pavement, boot heels drumming for a second on concrete before he shivered out, relaxing into death. Another soldier down, which meant Nat and the other members of her team were now outnumbered roughly three-to-one, including the invaders who had shown up uninvited at her target's home away from home.

Clear for the moment, Nat raced for the mansion's porch and cleared it in four strides, trying the front door's knob. Whoever last went through had taken time to lock it, so she blasted off the knob and deadbolt with her AK-9, then kicked the stout door open, dropping to a combat crouch before she crossed the threshold.

14

Grant Mahoney wasn't sure how he'd been separated from his brother. No matter how he searched the battlefield between gunfire exchanges, he could see no sign of Blake or any other member of their team.

At such a point, some soldiers might have panicked, but Mahoney had been through enough training and brutal life-or-death encounters that he'd learned to rein in self-destructive attitudes.

Immune to fear? Not even close. But he was past surrendering to it, prepared to battle through it and survive if that were possible.

This time, it looked felt like touch-and-go.

Mahoney thought of entering their target's house—a large one, but a comedown from the days when Pablo Escobar The First had ruled his global empire from Hacienda Nápoles at Puerto Triunfo, sprawling over eight square miles, boasting a Spanish colonial house; a sculpture park; a zoo filled with exotic animals including elephants, birds, giraffes, hippopotamuses and ostriches; a collection of classic cars and motorcycles; a private airport; a bullring, and a kart-racing track. Mounted atop the hacienda's entrance gate was a replica of the Piper PA-18 Super Cub airplane that flew Escobar's first shipment of cocaine to the United States.

It was amazing what a guy could do while pulling in $70 million per day.

If death had brought "hard times" to Escobar—or whoever in hell he was—the narcotrafficker still lived better than 95 percent of his fellow Colombians and he was on the rise.

Or had been, until tonight.

Mahoney finally decided he would skip searching the house. It felt more like a death trap than a hunting ground, and instinct told him that his target would be seeking to escape right now, taking off by any means available and leaving his men holding the bag, compelled to do or die on his behalf.

"Pablo," by any name, would be considering escape routes from the property right now, and since he couldn't risk running the gauntlet that his driveway had become, what did that leave?

Unless he had a time machine, that left a getaway by air. And where could he have stashed an aircraft but somewhere behind his house?

Jorge Torrenegra found his pilot in the kitchen, drinking his employer's Ron Viejo de Caldas Rum. He snatched the glass from Édgar's hand and hurled it toward the far wall, shattering the crystal.

"*¿Estas sobrio?*" he demanded.

Matiz cringed before his master. "*Sí, jefe.* Cold sober."

"Is the aircraft ready for takeoff?"

Matiz blinked once, then bobbed his head in the affirmative. "Fueled up and ready," he replied. "I only need to make the final flight check and run down the startup checklist. Fuel pressure, throttle, governor, hydraulics—"

"*¡Cállate!*" the man in charge cut off his flow of jargon. "I could read a *maldito* instruction manual for all of that. *¡Venga!* Let's go!"

The pilot blinked again, glancing around the kitchen as if seeking other passengers. "Is no one else coming, *Señor*?"

"They are preoccupied, *tonto*. We fly alone."

A jerky motion with his MP5K submachine gun put Édgar Matiz in motion toward the kitchen's back door exit, opening onto the patio, the swimming pool, and spacious yard beyond. There sat Jorge's Bell 525 Relentless chopper, its main rotors drooping as if the airship was sleeping.

Gunfire echoed from the front street side of the house as they emerged onto the patio, moved past the barbecue and swimming pool. Matiz glanced backward with a nervous look, until Torrenegra prodded him with his weapon's short muzzle, urging the pilot onward.

"*¡Prisa!*" Jorge snapped. "*¡Vamos!*"

"*Sí, jefe.*" Matiz picked up his pace, a shambling trot now, reaching the nearer of the helicopter's large rear sliding doors. He rolled it back and stood aside. Told his employer, "After you, *Señor.*"

"Just get it started," Torrenegra ordered, "and stop wasting time."

Chastened, the pilot climbed aboard and hustled toward the cockpit, strapped himself into his normal seat, and started flipping switches on the Bell's instrument panel. Torrenegra didn't understand the drill, nor did he care to learn it. All he wanted at that moment was to be airborne and leave his enemies behind.

Slamming the chopper's door and latching it, he moved to take a window seat facing the house. Confinement in the Bell's pressurized cabin muted sounds of battle from outside, dulling the *crack* of gunshots and the *whump* of high-explosive detonations. Watching out for adversaries, Torrenegra understood that he would never see this place again or call it home.

But if he managed to survive the night, he would press on, pursue his goal of mastery over the *llello* trade, and ultimately reap rewards that would eclipse his forebearer's splendid wealth.

If he survived.

If not…well, who would care in two weeks' time?

A skeptic when it came to any sort of afterlife, Jorge did not fear hellfire, and he certainly did not expect to walk on streets of hold in Heaven.

That thought almost made him chuckle as the helicopter's engines started droning, warming up in preparation for his great escape.

Natalie Karpin began to second-guess her entry to the manor house within a span of seconds, but by then she lacked the option of retreat. Gunfire was picking up outside, accompanied by shouts and screams. To top it off, someone discharged an RPG round—likely from the same weapon employed against her team at Avri Park that same night—and its detonation partially collapsed the manor house's entryway.

Her only path lay straight ahead now, with a Devil's choice of branching off upstairs or staying on the ground floor with its spreading swirl of smoke.

She doubted that the man impersonating Pablo Escobar would trap himself upstairs, so Natalie dismissed that option out of hand and moved on past a wall festooned with portraits toward a midpoint in the house, where corridors branched off to either side. Ahead, she guessed, must lie the dining room and kitchen, with an exit at the rear to serve the patio and pool she'd seen on Google Earth.

If phony Pablo went out through the back, what would he gain? Satellite photos showed the property was totally enclosed, with nothing to suggest a rear gate opening on woodland there. At least in theory, her man was no more likely to be scaling nine-foot walls crowned by a layer of jagged broken glass than any of his soldiers—and considering his estimated age, less likely to succeed than one of his younger *sicarios*.

Still…

Natalie was halfway to the kitchen, large enough to serve a thriving restaurant, when to gunmen emerged, both carrying Kalashnikovs, and stopped dead in their tracks on seeing her.

One challenged, "*¿Quién eres tú?*"

And while Nat didn't count Spanish among the five languages she spoke fluently, she recognized the tone, perhaps confusing her assailants as she answered, "Your worst nightmare."

In the split-second before they opened fire, she beat them two it, stroking short bursts from her AK-9 carbine from twenty feet or less. The soldier on her left dropped first, clutching his ventilated abdomen, blood gushing from between his fingers as he fell. The other tried to turn and run, taking her 9×39mm bullets in his right side, opening him up from hip to armpit, clamming him against the dining room's doorframe.

Scratch two more hostiles off the list.

Nat moved ahead more cautiously, taking her time, while conscious that she had little to spare. The posh estate might have no neighbors for a quarter mile or more, but with the racket going on outside, whoever was at home in any general direction would be on the phone by now, calling for cops, firefighters, maybe even army troops.

And if that weren't enough, from somewhere out beyond the house in back, she heard a helicopter's engines revving up toward takeoff. That could only mean one thing, one member of the household hauling ass away from there, and Natalie refused to let him slip away from her a second time.

Grim-faced, she sprinted down the corridor to reach the kitchen and its door leading outside.

"*¿Cuanto tiempo más?*" Jorge demanded of his pilot, seated in the Bell 525's cockpit.

"Not much longer, *jefe*," Édgar Matiz assured him, glancing nervously over his shoulder as if he expected to be shot for wasting precious time. "If I do not adjust the settings properly, we'll crash."

"And if you wait much longer it will make no difference, *cabron*. These *pinche bandidos* will be glad to kill us on the ground."

The pilot muttered something Torrenegra didn't catch, but he supposed that it was just as well. The panic he was in right now, the slightest backtalk could have set him off, and if he shot Matiz there would be no escape.

Instead, he sat and waited, fuming, while the chopper's rotors finally began revolving overhead, picking up speed. He saw a dark-haired woman exit from his kitchen, pausing briefly as she spied the helicopter revving up. He would have shot her down, or tried to, but the aircraft's window would not open, leaving him to mutter curses at his pilot, at his enemies, at Fate itself.

"For Christ's sake hurry up!" he bellowed at Édgar Matiz. "They're coming!"

"Just another moment now, *jefe*. We're almost ready."

Torrenegra clutched his MP5K with such force his knuckles throbbed, waiting to see if he would live or die.

Blake Mahoney met Reg Hardy in the midst of chaos, ducking slugs that swarmed around them like infuriated hornets.

"Came to join the party?" he asked Hardy.

"Wouldn't miss it for the bloody world."

"That's what we've got tonight, looks like."

As Blake was answering his teammate he squeezed off a three-round AK-9 burst that sent one of phony Pablo's gunmen sprawling to the grass.

"Where are the others?" Hardy asked, raising his voice to make it audible over the battle's din.

"Damned if I know. Sticking together hasn't worked so far."

"Where are you headed, then?" Reg asked.

"Around back," Blake advised. "Hear that?"

A heartbeat later, Hardy nodded. "Sounds just like a whirlybird."

"I'd give you a cigar but I'm fresh out."

"About to lose our man again, are we?"

"I'm sure *he* thinks so," said Mahoney, "but I don't intend to make it easy for him."

"Happy to help out with that," Hardy replied.

As they moved out along the stately home's south side, a loud explosion rocked the house behind them, shattering stonework and wood.

"I wouldn't mind having that RPG right now," Blake said.

"No time to hunt and fetch," Hardy reminded him.

Scowling, Blake said, "You got that right. Let's move!"

Finally, Jorge Torrenegra felt the helicopter lurch, then start to rise. A brief surge of excitement died within him as the woman standing on his back steps moved to intercept the Bell 525, the muzzle flashes from her automatic weapon painting bright pinpricks across his retinas.

"*¡Prisa!*" he bawled out toward the cockpit. "Hurry! They are firing at us!"

"Lifting off," Édgar Matiz called back to him and made it happen, handling the Bell's controls as if they were embarking on a pleasure flight to view the neon lights of Medellín.

A rifle bullet plunked against the helicopter's fuselage, immediately followed by another. When a third one cracked his plexiglass window, Jorge felt panic rising in his throat and threatening to choke him.

"*¡Vamos! ¡Ve ahora!*" he cried out, embarrassed by his voice's high-pitched squeal. "Go now!"

"We're off," Matiz reported, and they were, rising with glacial speed above the lawn that bore impressions from the helicopter's landing gear.

Across the lawn where Torrenegra once had sunbathed in the nude, his female adversary was advancing at a run, still firing steadily. If any of her bullets struck the engine housing or the rotor cables…

They could still escape, Jorge believed, but they were swiftly running out of time. Why were the Bell's twin GE turboshaft engines taking so long to speed them out of rifle range?

Rafael Bernal slammed a 40mm high-explosive round into another of the vehicles that had delivered raiders to his master's doorstep, watching as the black sedan erupted into roiling flame and smoke.

No one had been inside the car, but blasting it prevented more of Pablo's enemies from trying to escape the trap they'd laid out for themselves. Striking against a larger force on unfamiliar ground was foolish.

Now their foes would learn that it was suicide in fact.

Bernal fed another HE cannister into his M203 launcher's breech and snapped the sliding mechanism shut, prepared to fire again, when he was momentarily distracted by the sound of helicopter engines revving into takeoff mode behind the manor house. He'd been expecting that, of course, but when the sound came to his ears over the clash of combat, something clicked inside his head.

His master was deserting him, along with all the other young men who had pledged themselves to serve him even unto death. Where sacrifice had seemed a noble prospect only moments earlier, it now struck Rafael as gross betrayal on the part of his *padrino*, godfather of the cartel they'd built together and responsible as such for all the Medellín *sicarios* under his leadership.

Jorge was fleeing to preserve himself and leaving all the rest of them behind, something the true Pablo would not have contemplated, even in the final hours of his life. That Pablo Escobar had given back to his community—constructing schools, hospitals, sports venues—and elevating locals mired in poverty to status in Colombian society beyond their wildest childhood fantasies.

Of course, some died along the way and others went to prison, all inevitable in the life of narcotrafficking, but when they fell or were incarcerated, each loyal servant of the Escobar cartel knew that his family would be provided for and never want for anything.

Tonight, the charlatan impersonating Pablo had betrayed all that—or would, if Rafael permitted him to get away with it.

Sobbing in anger and frustration, Rafael Bernal turned his back on the invaders storming Jorge's manse and ran around the east end of the house, intent on stopping Jorge Torrenegra's selfish getaway.

Grant Mahoney reached the backyard of their target's home away from home as Natalie Karpin unleashed another burst of AK-9 fire at the rising Bell 525 Relentless. He could see her bullets scar the chopper's fuselage, but it still seemed to earn its brand name, shrugging off the small insult and gaining altitude, ascending out of range.

Grant cursed and heard it echoed by his brother, trailed by Reg Hardy, arriving on the scene too late to intervene. Around the northeast corner of the manor house, Stan Dartnell joined them, then stopped dead, eyes on the chopper, spewing profanity.

All this for nothing, while their mark prepared to show them all his back and disappear to who knew where.

A howling suddenly distracted all of them, drawing their eyes away from the escaping whirlybird. A slim *sicario* with greasy hair falling around his shoulders, carrying an M4/M203 combo weapon, stopped short in his tracks, aiming his weapon skyward, shouting Spanish epithets over the helicopter's noise.

Four SFX members swung carbines toward the new arrival, but Grant's voice forestalled their firing.

"Hold on for a second, people."

As they watched, the ranting gunman fired his 40mm launcher at the Bell 525, allowing for the range and calculating the parabola of its trajectory with aid from rifle attachment's ladder sight. At first, Mahoney doubted he could score a hit, but the retreating chopper had not covered the 380 yards required to slip beyond effective range as yet, and just when Grant was ready to dismiss the shot as wasted effort, an explosion rocked the airship, shearing off its tail.

Without its tail rudder, the Bell Relentless went into a spin and looped back toward the house it had been trying to escape. Mahoney couldn't see the pilot grappling with his antitorque and pitch controls, but he was clearly losing it. In seconds flat the Bell was roaring back toward the mansion's veranda, nosing steeply downward on a dead-end course to impact.

No one on the SFX team needed orders to disperse. The scattered like zoo patrons when a snarling panther leaps from its enclosure and begins to run amok, panicked and lashing out on every side.

The Bell 525 nose-dived into the backyard swimming pool, raising a twenty-foot tsunami wave that washed over the tiled deck, toppling flimsy poolside furniture and sweeping it away. The wave broke against "Pablo's" tall broad brick barbecue, its remnants flowing on to lap against the rec room's sliding doors.

A heartbeat after impact, the twin engines blew, immediately followed by the Bell's fuel tanks. The swimming pool where narcotraffickers and naked women once cavorted instantly became a seething lake of fire, bright flames devouring the helicopter's broken fuselage before it slowly settled underwater, raising clouds of smoke and steam.

No one was getting out of there alive.

The shooter with the M203 launcher realized he had a hostile audience and swung around to face the SFX team with his M4 carbine. All five of the squad's commandos opened up on him in unison, spinning him through a crazy dervish whirl, a ragdoll figure coming apart at the seams before it collapsed in a heap and lay still.

"We done here?" Blake Mahoney asked the group.

Out front, where firefights sputtered on, combatants shouted, breaking off and rallying to find out what was happening behind the smoking manor house.

"Seems like it," Grant agreed. "Somebody have a scaling rope?"

"I still have mine," Reg Hardy answered. "Didn't need it, coming through the busted gate."

"That works for me," Grant said. "Last one over the wall buys the first round."

15

"Are you at risk by coming here, *Señor*?"

Brigadier General Raúl Sandino phrased the question casually, or tried to, but his visitor did not appear to mind. Instead, the well-dressed *gringo* shrugged, cocked one eyebrow, and raised his right hand with its first finger extended, swiveling to make tight circles in the air.

"Are we secure?" Sandino easily interpreted the silent question. "*Pero por supuesto.* But of course. No one may eavesdrop here without my knowing it."

"Is that supposed to put my mind at ease?" asked Preston Chandler of the DEA.

"Suspicious minds," Sandino said, smiling as he sat down behind his spacious desk. "You have my word, *Señor.* How do you say it? Cross my heart and hope to die?"

"That's not just an expression where I come from," Chandler cautioned. "It comes true from time to time."

"As we experience ourselves," Sandino said. "More often, I believe, than you find happening in Washington."

Chandler carried on as if his host had not spoken. "Because if somebody *was* taping this and planned to use it later for his personal advantage, he might be surprised to find what else is already on tape, ready to leak at need."

Sandino frowned and spread his hands. "May we not speak as men who trust each other after all this time?"

"You mean as colleagues? Allies?" Chandler asked him. "How would that work in the real world?"

"Is it not already working?" asked the brigadier. "Has not our problem been resolved?"

"One may have been," the DEA man granted. "Now that Pablo What's-his-name is back on ice for good."

"Thanks to your contractors, with some help from *Don* Joaquín Cardenas Sanchez in Jalisco, eh?"

"That one's next on my list," Chandler replied. "Once he's out of the way, you've got a clean shot at coordinating shipments northward through your own contacts."

"And you bank your percentage as agreed. *¿No es así?*"

"As we agreed, that's right."

"Regrettably, I cannot help you with the work you plan in Mexico."

"I've got it covered. There's a friendly colonel with National Guard in Guadalajara who can handle things up there."

As both men present in the office knew full well, Mexico had suffered problems with its federal police on par with nations farther south, and worse than some. Originally organized in 1928, the first batch of *federales* underwent a cosmetic makeover in 1999, renamed the Federal Ministerial Police, then "Ministerial" was dropped ten years later, then the Federal Police was finally dissolved in 2019, President Andrés López Obrador citing its hopeless institutional corruption by competing drug cartels. Today, enforcement of most federal laws fell to the Mexican National Guard, while certain groundwork was conducted by agents of a Federal Investigative Agency based in Mexico City.

In short, a literal Mexican stand-off with feds versus feds, most with their hands out in quest of *mordida*.

"So," Sandino said, "I only need to organize the Los Urabeños and the Mesa Family, together with the Santa Cruz Cartel's shipments transported from Bolivia?"

"Affirmative," Chandler replied. "And then we're Parker Brothers, *mi amigo.*"

"*¿Cómo es eso?*"

When Sandino looked confused, the DEA man graced him with an understanding smile and asked, "You ever play 'Monopoly' when you were younger, General?"

"The board game? No. My parents could spare no *dinero* for frivolities."

"Too bad," said Chandler. "When we have all out pieces squared away, we'll have Boardwalk and Park Place sewed up tight and covered with a shitload of those little green houses."

Sandino's blank look still bespoke a lack of understanding.

Chandler tried once more. "Figure we bank a couple million dollars each whenever one of our loads passes 'Go' and makes it to the States or overseas."

"Ah. *Mucho dinero,* eh?"

"And then some," Chandler said.

"In which case, I'm inviting you to lunch—that is, if you have time to spare?"

"I've got all afternoon," Chandler replied. "Meeting with our ambassador at six, an update on our progress with the drug war, then a dinner at the embassy."

"I have a booking for us at the Barbaro Cocina Primitiva. Have you tried it?"

"Never even heard of it," Chandler confessed.

"It's rated as the top steakhouse in Medellín," Sandino said. "The cut its chef calls 'Tomahawk' is said to weigh one thousand grams, although I have not sampled it myself."

"A kilo? What the hell. We only live once, right?"

Sandino had to laugh at that. "Except for Pablo Escobar," he said.

"And look how that worked out for him. Poor bastard's dead again."

They rose to leave, pausing while Brigadier Sandino double-locked his private office door behind them. Working at her desk in the reception room, his secretary glanced up from her laptop long enough to flash a fetching smile.

The two men breezed on past her, General Sandino in his uniform, Chandler in a three-piece Dolce & Gabbana tailored to conceal his love handles. While waiting for the elevator to arrive, nobody else within earshot, Chandler asked his companion, "So, you plan to lead another Cartel of the Suns?"

Sandino's shrug was casual. "If so, I do not wish to see it end the same way as in Venezuela."

"That's an object lesson to us all," Chandler agreed. "Deal with the politicians if it's unavoidable, but never trust one in a pinch."

"Amen to that," Sandino said.

The car arrived and took them smoothly down to the ground floor. Downstairs, they exited into a spacious lobby teeming with men and women in uniform, rubbing shoulders with others in suits. Chandler saw no one sporting casual attire and reckoned that defendants facing trial were either channeled through another entrance or were coming up from basement cells, wearing jumpsuits and chains.

Outside, it was a short walk to the parking lot, surrounded by a chain-link fence with razor wire on top, its gate secured by two corporals armed with IMI Galil assault rifles, purchased from Tel Aviv to arm the military, augmenting the army's cache of other weapons made in Israel, the United States and Germany.

They waited for Sandino's limousine, then climbed into the backseat while his appointed driver held the door. Raúl did not immediately recognize the man standing before him, so he asked, "*¿Dónde está el cabo Gómez?*"

"Sir," the driver answered him, "the corporal has temporarily been reassigned."

Sandino frowned at that. "*¿Reasignado?* Nothing serious, I hope. He's served me well."

"A personal concern, Sir. Sadly, a bereavement in the family."

"*¡Qué lastima!*" With the expression of condolence, Brigadier Sandino put the absent noncom out of mind and told the new man, "We are going to the Barbaro Cocina Primitiva. Do you know it, Corporal?"

"Yes, Sir. In Laureles, on Carrera 76, the second floor."

"Perfecto. Let's be on our way, then."

Snug inside the limousine, despite a Perspex window raised between the unfamiliar driver and themselves, Sandino and the DEA man held their conversation to a minimum, restricted to banalities. Beside the new man in the driver's seat, both knew the car could not be scanned for bugs as regularly or as thoroughly as General Sandino's private office.

Fifteen minutes passed before Sandino felt the first faint stirring of alarm. He keyed the intercom and asked the man behind the wheel, "Is this the right way, Corporal?"

"I may have missed a turn, Sir. I will stop for just a moment and consult the street guide."

Suiting words to action, he pulled over in the middle of a seedy-looking block, then pressed a button on the central console, lowering the window, turning back to face Sandino and his lunch guest from the States.

Holding a pistol leveled in his hand.

"*¿Cuál es el significado de este ultraje, cabo?*" General Sandino snapped, shifting from curious to furious in a split-second.

At his side, Chandler already knew the meaning of this outrage, as the brigadier had called it.

"Grant Mahoney? What in God's name are you doing here?"

"Just taking out the trash," replied the president of SFX.

"Explain yourself!" Chandler demanded.

"Sure, why not? Although we haven't got a lot of time," Mahoney said. "At least, *you* don't."

The sinking feeling in his gut told Chandler all he had to know. Dropping the pose of injured innocence, he asked Mahoney, "So, what tipped you off?"

"Your phone tips nailed it down," Grant said. "Blake had your phone hacked from the day you visited our office. You were cagey for a while, but toward the end there... well, you couldn't stop yourself from helping things along, could you? First tipping us to where we'd find our man, then calling up the Mexicans right afterward. That's what I call a careless move."

Disgusted with himself for making such a rookie move, taking the SFX team for a crew of simple-minded mercenaries, Chandler shook his head. Smiled ruefully.

Sandino, on the other hand, was keeping up his act. "What does he mean, *Señor* Preston? Have you deceived us all?"

"Nice try," Mahoney told the brigadier, "but it won't wash."

"*¿No se lava? ¿Qué significa eso?*"

"And now he's playing dumb. "*¿No hablas inglés, general?*" He actually laughed at that, as if enjoying it.

And shot Sandino in the face.

Mahoney's weapon had a sound suppressor screwed onto its muzzle, but at such close range, it had no measurable impact on the slug's muzzle velocity. Blood spattered Chandler's face and stained his custom-tailored suit.

"Okay," the DEA man said, unable to disguise the tremor in his tone. "Where do we go from here?"

"I'm headed back to San Diego," Grant replied. "You've got a reservation at the morgue."

"And you expect to get away with this? Icing a chief

assistant deputy director of the DEA?"

"A *dirty* chief assistant deputy director," Grant reminded him.

"Prove it!" Chandler demanded.

"Well, you've got a little something there on your lapel, for starters," said Mahoney. But the dirt I have in mind is on its way to Washington by email as we speak, routed through Bogotá, Guadalajara—with a copy to *Don* Cardenas—and a ricochet out of Ukraine to keep the NSA guessing."

"My people will look into this!"

"I'm counting on it."

"You won't get away with it!"

"Smart money says they'll be too busy looking into you and your affairs."

"Your company is eyebrow-deep in all of this," warned Chandler.

"At the DEA's request," Mahoney said. "We've got five witnesses, a signed contract, and your down payment from the agency, all backing a legitimate request for an investigation off the books. Whatever happened after that to foul you up with underworld competitors, it's not our problem."

"Do you *seriously* think my agency, my peers, will let this slide like it was nothing? I've been working toward my present post for twenty-seven years!"

"And now they'll have to question every bust you ever made, along with any deals you cut along the way, all the informants you promoted. My guess, headquarters will gladly sweep your mess under the rug and hope nobody notices at CNN or Fox."

"Sounds like you've got it all worked out, smart guy."

"As far as possible. I'll take my chances on the rest."

"Well, then, screw you! You may as well—"

The pistol's sound suppressor made another muffled *pop* and silenced Preston Chandler's final words. His head snapped back, and this time it was his blood spurting onto Brigadier Sandino, not that the Colombian policeman was aware of it.

Mahoney stowed his piece, walked back around the limousine and patted down both corpses, pocketing their cell phones although neither had been switched on or recording in their final moments. That done, he stepped clear and closed the back door, took a burner from his pocket, and punched up the only preset number it contained—another throwaway that Nat Karpin was carrying.

"All done?" she asked him.

"Time to go," Mahoney said.

"Two minutes."

It was more like ninety seconds when she pulled up in one of their airport rental cars and Grant climbed in beside her, settling in the shotgun seat.

"Any last words?" she asked.

After he'd snapped the burner phone in half and pulled its SIM card, Grant patted his borrowed uniform's breast pocket. "Chandler expressing outrage to the bitter end, but not denying anything. After we put it through voice-alteration on my side, it goes to the director's office by FedEx, out of a drop box somewhere safe."

"Las Vegas?" Natalie suggested.

"Good enough. I wouldn't send Stan, though, until the heat dies down."

"He's likely to have something else on tap."

"So, what about the second million?" she inquired.

"Thought we might wait until they're finished wading through his paperwork. Somebody's bound to come and ask about it. If we haven't got the rest, I'll ask about it casually, surprised as hell to hear the job went south on Chandler."

"So, we're done in Medellín?"

"Feels done to me. Did you have something else in mind to follow up on?"

"What about Jalisco?" Natalie replied.

"We can't start chasing drug cartels around the map unless somebody's paying for it, and I'd like to take a breather from it anyway."

"Got something else on tap?"

"With extra money in the bank, maybe one of those trafficking outfits that you've been looking into."

"Maybe," Natalie replied, not sounding quite persuaded.

"We've got time to wait and see," Grant said. "No urgency to grab another job before some R and R."

"Sounds good to me," she readily agreed.

"Maybe a little traveling with Blake, no strings attached."

The glance she shot at him would easily have withered lesser men.

"Don't push it," she cautioned. "A joke can only go so far."

If You Liked This, You Might Like: Blood Sport: Special Agents Flynn and Tanner, FBI (VICAP Book 1)

Los Angeles is city primeval, home base for the sociopathic elite. Charles Manson. The Hillside Strangler. And now—the Reaper. He hunts at night terrorizing whole families at gunpoint, mutilating and finally slaughtering them. Dozens of victims. No survivors. No Clues.

Special Agents Joe Flynn and Martin Tanner, are highly trained members of the Federal Bureau of Investigation's Violent Criminal Apprehension Program. But the Reaper never leaves a trace. Flynn and Tanner can do nothing except pace in the shadows of the sleeping city waiting for the Reaper to strike again.

The case files of Special Agents Flynn and Tanner are a scorching record of brutal crime. Their Los Angeles is an urban nightmare ruled by psychotic lords of violence. But VICAP agents are tough and resourceful—and they never give up.

Thought this series is fiction, VICAP is a real organization initially conceived in the late 1960s when the crimes of the Boston Strangler, Charles Manson, and other "motiveless" killers began to make national headlines.

AVAILABLE NOW

ABOUT THE AUTHOR

A California native, Michael Newton has published 215 books under his own name and various pseudonyms since 1977. He began writing professionally as a "ghost" for author Don Pendleton on the best-selling Executioner series and continues his work on that series today. With 104 episodes published to date, Newton has nearly tripled the number of Mack Bolan novels completed by creator Pendleton himself.

Newton's first book under his own name was Monsters, Mysteries and Man (1979), a survey of unexplained phenomena for younger readers. While 156 of Newton's published books have been novels—including westerns, political thrillers and psychological suspense—he is best known for nonfiction, primarily true crime and reference books.